INSIDE A PRIVATE ROOM
AT BENTWELL'S . . .

Oleo opened the door and stepped into the antiseptic-smelling room. The girl jumped to her feet. He leapt forward and struck her arm with his gloved hand. For an instant, nothing happened. Then the pain of the glove's contact made itself known; that area of her arm quickly became a red pulp of bleeding flesh.

She cried, screamed, sobbed, babbled hysterically, thrashed about on the bed, then finally, turning away from him, tried to find a way through the clean white walls with her fingernails.

He stood beside the bed admiring his handiwork, enjoying the tortured whimpering noises escaping her lips. He removed his jumpsuit slowly.

Oleo was ready to begin.

CRYSTAL PHOENIX

MICHAEL BERLYN

CRYSTAL PHOENIX
A Bantam Book | June 1980

ISBN 0-553-13468-X

Published simultaneously in the United States and Canada

Bantam Books are published by Bantam Books, Inc. Its trade-
mark, consisting of the words "Bantam Books" and the por-
trayal of a bantam, is Registered in U.S. Patent and Trademark
Office and in other countries. Marca Registrada. Bantam
Books, Inc., 666 Fifth Avenue, New York, New York 10019.

PRINTED IN THE UNITED STATES OF AMERICA

0 9 8 7 6 5 4 3 2 1

For all the young punks,
soon to be old punks,
and for M. M. McClung.

CRYSTAL PHOENIX

She smiled straight at m— and I knew, even
if I would have hidden it if a— you any of it, that
she was as one had ever been. In that moment of that
I was I was all along, and was of it. I— maybe, both
of it. I had. I we emotionally — I'd been aware until

1

Albert "Oleo" Johnson stood in the middle of his den and looked around carefully. The walls were lined with shelves and display cases from floor to ceiling, all filled with antique and baroque instruments of pain, torture, and death. A hidden projector flashed images of great wars onto the ceiling to musical fanfares heralding great feats, great deaths, great pain. There were two old-fashioned electric chairs for Oleo to sit in, two coffins for lounging, and a turn-of-the-century hospital bed complete with height and angle controls for real relaxing.

It was a comfortable room.

Oleo was a tall man with olive skin and an equine face. His feet were very large, as were his hands, ears, nose, and legs. At 213 centimeters, everything about him had to be large.

He looked on every shelf, studying each weapon, pondering the vast array of tools from which he would have to choose one, and only one, to use on tonight's victim. It was a difficult choice.

Last night he had used a single-edged razor blade—an extremely costly item he'd turned up while browsing at an auction. None of the other effects had been worth anything, and the only real bidding had been for the razor blades. Just by looking at the items up for bid, Oleo had known the dead person had been a one-timer, unable to afford a life-crystal while he'd still been alive.

But the razor blades had come in handy. Oleo's victim had been old and wheezing, a half-dead geriatric case who died well before Oleo had had a chance to finish the job. He cursed himself when the old man died—what fun was there in skinning a corpse? If he had used both hands for the skinning he might have gotten further.

Oleo had needed one hand to masturbate. He'd barely managed orgasm, and that had been only marginal; if it hadn't been for the old geezer's death rattles, Oleo would have gone home tired, lonely, and frustrated. Well, that wouldn't happen this time. No, not this time, Oleo thought.

Acupuncture needles? Perhaps, but too much depended on the age and condition of the victim. If he turned out to be young, the needles would be next to worthless. Unless, of course, the person had a phobia for needles. No—too much of a longshot.

Oleo sighed, and rubbed the side of his long, fleshy nose. He took his time, and looked in every case once more, in every corner of the room. He ignored the guns. They were good weapons to use, but only under the right conditions: you had to be screwing someone and pull the trigger and blow their brains out at exactly the right moment. Too much depended on timing, and timing was not one of Oleo's long suits.

It was a difficult decision indeed.

He took a glove from one of the dust-covered glass cases and slipped it on. It smelled of old leather. Its fur lining was silky smooth, warm and comforting next to his skin. He flexed his hand a few times to stretch out the seams, then turned it over, opening it so he could see the thousands of tiny razor-sharp pins that covered the palm and fingers. He could puncture a large portion of his victim's skin by slapping him. Hit often enough, there would be copious amounts of blood and pain. Hit more, the victim would bleed to death—a slow, painful, vicious way for some procurer's client to die.

Nice, Oleo thought. Nice indeed.

He felt a tingle of excitement start in his groin. He hoped it would be a woman tonight. Surely, someone at Bentwell's would have what he was looking for. It was close to 4 A.M. and there wouldn't be many procurers still there, but Oleo did not want to wait another day.

He took an aviator's jump suit down from one of the shelves, shook it out to get rid of the dust and stale smell, then unzipped its front. He took the glove off, and slipped the jump suit on over his clothes.

There was a chance that one of the procurers would be able to set him up with a victim immediately. If another angel had cancelled and left the procurer with an expectant client, then Oleo would be ready. The jump suit would protect his clothing. He would drive to the Center, take care of pleasure, take off the jump suit, drive to his office, then take care of business. All he would need was a few stimulants to get him through the day.

He folded the glove and slipped it into his pocket, right next to the permanent membership card for Bentwell's.

There was only one thing left to do before he could leave: update his life-crystal. It would take less than a minute, but it would ensure that his personality and memories would be recorded, and would survive the night, even if his body didn't.

2

"Mr. Lange?" someone asked, tapping Dennis on the shoulder. He turned away from the crowd. "Mr. Lange?"

Dennis nodded and smiled with a genuineness that had taken years to perfect. "Yes?"

The man Dennis faced was tall and thin, wearing a too-loose conservative suit easily four months out of style. He had a thin mustache, short, wavy, brown hair, and bushy eyebrows. His nose took a sharp downward hook, like a puffin's bill. He held his drink before his stomach with both hands, as if he didn't know what to do with the half-empty glass. His nails were carefully manicured.

Pencil pusher, Dennis thought. Probably low-rent, but with distinct possibilities. A one-shot angel.

"My name is Howard Warren." He held out his hand.

Dennis shook it, then casually wiped his hand on his pants to get rid of the cold, clammy feeling. "Call me Dennis. What can I do for you?"

"You're a procurer, aren't you?" Warren asked, blushing.

Dennis couldn't believe it. Warren had lowered his gaze, and was staring at the floor, awkwardly shifting his weight from foot to foot.

"I am," Dennis said, glancing at the red disc pinned to his chest; it was still there, so there was no reason for Warren to have asked if he were a procurer. It had to be the man's first time.

"Well, Mr. Lange. . . ."

"Just call me Dennis, okay?"

Warren nodded. "Okay, Dennis. I, uhm . . . I'm not quite sure . . . how to . . . what to. . . ."

"There's nothing to be embarrassed about," Dennis said, smiling his priceless, cultured, genuine smile. "You're just looking for a little companionship, right?"

The man nodded and leaned closer. "Is there someplace a little more . . . private where we could, uhm, talk? One of the niches?"

Dennis looked around Bentwell's crowded main lounge. It was the size of a large hotel lobby with a high, beamed ceiling, gaudy chandeliers, plush but well-worn chairs lining the two long walls, and a bar along the short wall opposite the main doors. The place smelled old, deep and musty, overlaid by sweet sweat and perfumes. The people were drunk, drugged, or most probably both; laughing and giggling, waving their hands, their fingers finding other fingers, other hands, other thighs; and all the while all of them talking, talking, talking, roaring like a thousand holosets tuned to different programs.

Dennis knew that Warren was going to be good. He could feel it deep down in his gut, and that feeling hadn't been wrong yet.

"Sure," Dennis said. "Let's find one that's empty."

The people before him formed a constantly shifting wall that went back, layer after layer, like a marauding army. His wife, Kira, was in there somewhere. She was probably talking to some nicely wrapped, steroid- and silicone-packed, selectively impotent side of beef. Every time he took her along to Bentwell's she ended up drunk or stoned to the point where she had to be carried to the car. Bentwell was usually the cause: he wanted Kira, but she would never allow that. She couldn't stand the man, for reasons ranging from his pudgy profile and double chins to the stale-smelling cloud which hovered around him. Still, he owned the place, and Dennis couldn't afford to alienate him.

"Follow me," Dennis told Warren.

He pushed his way into the jumbled mass of bodies, heading for the nearest plastic niche. The first one was taken; a man and woman were having sex on its floor. He pushed his way further into the crowd and found one that was empty. Warren stepped inside and Dennis was about to follow when he felt someone grab him by the elbow. He turned around.

A young woman in skin-tight bolero pants and a low-cut jersey top which exposed her breasts stood before him. He scowled. It was Mara Frank; she met his gaze as she sipped from a highball glass. She was tall, just a few centimeters shorter than Dennis, statuesque, had long straight black hair, and was nothing but trouble. She, too, wore the red disc of the procurer.

"What do you want?" Dennis demanded.

"We have to talk," she said.

"Not now. Leave me alone. I'm busy."

"Busy with my angel," she said.

"Your angel, huh? All right. Wait a minute." He leaned into the small booth and smiled at Warren. "I'll be with you in a moment, okay? Do you mind waiting?"

Warren smiled and shook his head.

"Good. I'll be right back." He closed the door to the niche and faced Mara Frank.

Her face was classically beautiful, as smooth and firm and flawless as her breasts, but as cold as a love affair gone bad. Long Roman nose, heavy, pouting lips, high cheekbones, careful but flashy makeup. Even though every part of her looked thirty, her deep-set brown eyes were hard, bitter, and empty; she was about to hit thirty for the third time.

"Well?" he asked.

"That's Warren in there, Lange, and he's my angel. He approached Freddie and me, and we were talking a deal."

"He didn't sign, did he?"

She shook her head. "He was ours, though. Freddie and I worked on him. We put a lot of time in him. If you leave him alone, he'll come back over to us."

Dennis sighed. "Listen, Mara, I didn't have a thing to do with it. He came to me; I didn't go to him. If you two cleaned up your act and conducted your business like it should be conducted, then maybe you'd—"

"Shove it," Mara said. "I don't need one of your shit lectures. I want Warren back."

Dennis shrugged. "Sorry, Mara. This is business. And every angel means money to me. I'm not about to pass one up just because you feel he's yours."

She threw her glass to the floor. "He's ours, Lange."

Dennis opened the door to the niche. "Then go inside and talk to him. Be my guest. See if he wants to come with you now."

She looked as though she wanted to rip his heart out and feed it to him. She spun around and melted into the noisy crowd. Dennis stood there a moment, shaking his head, trying to understand Mara. A few weeks ago, she and her husband Freddie had been pressuring him to become partners. Dennis had refused. He was a good procurer; he didn't need people such as Freddie and Mara Frank dragging his business down to their level. Now, it was a different kind of pressure, a more annoying tack. It was hard to understand; Dennis and Freddie had once been friends.

Dennis's angels, his patrons, were willing to pay the high rates he charged for his clients because they knew he would deliver the best. What had Freddie and Mara ever delivered but trouble? Dennis knew that his angels and clients would flee like a swarm of frightened rats if he ever joined up with the Franks. His clients trusted him with more than their lives; they trusted him with their future lives, their reconstructions.

He walked into the niche. Warren was sitting on the chair as though it were carved out of ice, smoothing down his little mustache in an automatic movement.

"Sorry for the delay. Now, what exactly did you have in mind?" Dennis asked.

Warren blushed again and stared at his shoes. "I thought maybe a...woman...pretty, if possible...."

"And very afraid," Dennis said.

"Why, why yes. Yes."

Dennis nodded. He knew the type. They scrimped and saved for years, then blew all their money on one evening in a small white room with some procurer's client.

"Why me, Mr. Warren? There are a lot of procurers walking around Bentwell's. And I understand you talked to at least the Franks."

Warren wet his lips with a flick of his tongue. "This, uhm, this is the, uhm ... the first time I've ever been here, Mr. Lange."

"Dennis."

"Dennis. One of the bartenders said to talk to you before I signed anything. The Franks were really try-

8

ing to pressure me. I got wary, so I came to talk to you."

Dennis nodded. Warren seemed to be loosening up some. "I'm glad you did. There are all kinds of procurers in Bentwell's. Are you sure you want to do something like this? I mean it *is* expensive, and—"

Someone was standing in the doorway. He looked up and saw Mara Frank, hands on hips, glaring at him. Dennis got up to close the door. That was one way to get rid of her. She stepped inside before he reached the switch.

"What is it, Mara?" Dennis demanded.

"We're not through talking yet."

"Oh, yes, we are."

She stood there staring, breathing calmly.

Dennis sighed. Was this the way it was going to be from now on? Mara walking over to bother him as soon as he started talking to an angel or client? "Wait for me outside. I'll be with you in a minute."

"Now," Mara said.

He wanted to smash her face, practice a veteran angel's technique on her, but took a few deep breaths and turned to Warren instead. There were lots of other procurers walking around—Warren might not wait. But this thing with Mara had to be settled now, or it would probably happen with other angels. "Do you mind, Mr. Warren?"

Warren looked like he did mind, and was on the verge of getting up. "Well...."

"I'll only be a minute. I'd appreciate it if you could wait."

He turned and strode out of the niche. Mara followed. He wheeled around and stared into her eyes. "Now what's this all about?" he demanded.

She shrugged. "I just came by to make you an offer," she said in her innocent, smooth voice.

He nodded his head slowly, breathing through his nose, stomach muscles tight, teeth clamped together. "An offer, Mara? An offer?"

"Yeah. A partnership."

"What are you, insane?" he shouted. "I've told you both before: not with me! I'm not interested and I'll never be interested. Leave me alone." He realized he'd been shouting and took a deep breath, glancing around to see if he had attracted any unwanted attention. No one was staring.

He thought he spotted Kira, though, and swore silently. Mara turned and glanced in that direction; a gleam lit her eyes and the corners of her mouth crept upward almost imperceptibly.

"How's your wife, Dennis? Have you discussed this deal with her? Perhaps Kira will be more receptive to our offer," Mara said.

He leveled a finger at her. "You leave Kira out of this. I don't even want you talking to her. I'm warning you—stay away from her."

Mara grinned. "Watch it, Dennis. Your dominance pattern is showing and it's not very complimentary." She laughed. "I'll stay away, but I can't promise what Freddie will do. You know how impulsive he is."

He moved closer to her, close enough to smell her bittersweet perfume. His eyes narrowed to slits, and the muscles in his cheeks stood out in relief. "You tell him this. Tell him if he so much as looks at her the wrong way, he'll regret it."

She arched her eyebrows in mock surprise. "Giving orders now? Going to have me blackballed? Thrown out of Bentwell's?" She laughed in his face. "Or maybe Bentwell made you a partner, and you'll just throw me out yourself."

Warren had come out of the niche and was standing in the doorway. Lines of worry etched his forehead and he looked like he was about to say something. Dennis figured he had heard the last few comments and was working on a parting comment of his own. Nothing was going right.

Kira was less than five meters away, squirming and weaving through the crowd toward him, closing fast. Bentwell was waddling along behind, bouncing off people, tripping over his toga every other step, too far gone to close the distance.

"Dennis?" Kira shouted.

He turned back to Warren. Mara had left. "I'm sorry, Mr. Warren. Things aren't usually this bad. It seems like we're not going to get a chance to do much talking right now." He dug a business card out of his pocket. "Here. Why don't you give me a call and we can—"

"Dennis," Kira said, right by his side, hanging onto his elbow. "That Bentwell's been—who's this guy?" she asked, staring at Warren.

"His name is Howard Warren. Mr. Warren, this is my wife, Kira."

She was wearing a long, flowing, wispy gown that Dennis had picked out for her. He knew what the ethereal dress could do to the libidos of people like Bentwell or Warren. She was blonde, her hair cut shorter than fashion dictated, and slender; the kind of woman who should have exuded sex but looked too naive to know anything about it. A girl grown into a woman who hadn't realized it yet.

Warren nodded and smiled.

Kira shook her head and looked at the man as though he were human sewage. "What's your preference, Mr. Warren? Machine guns? Knives? Ptomaine poisoning?"

"Kira!" Dennis grabbed her elbow. She winced. "I'm sorry, Mr. Warren. My wife seems to have over-indulged."

"Hey!" Kira squealed, cutting off Warren's reply. She spun around to face Bentwell. "Keep your hands to yourself, fat boy!"

was flesh and fat, his cheeks small jowls. His eyes
Bentwell was too drunk to take offense. His face

11

were glassy, and a small trail of spittle crept from the corner of his mouth. "Come on, Kira," he pleaded. "I won't do anything to hurt you. I promise. Please?"

Dennis turned back to Warren but the lanky man had used the distraction to slip away into the crowd and the noise. He could have gone after him, but that would have meant leaving Kira alone with Bentwell. Besides, if Warren wanted to use his services, he would get in touch—he had the business card. There was no sense chasing the man. He turned back to Kira.

Bentwell was all over her, smothering her in layers of fat and saliva, grabbing and kissing whatever he could. Kira was doing her best, hitting with her free hand, kicking his ankles and shins.

"Enough!" Dennis yelled, yanking her out of Bentwell's grasp. "We're going home, Kira. Good night, Peter."

Bentwell leered, swaying precariously, dazed, groping at air.

Dennis pulled Kira through the throng, heading for the main doors. There had been no business for him at Bentwell's; the place was getting worse and worse. He could have waited for the late rush of angels that took place half an hour before closing, but the confrontation with Mara, and then Kira's comments, were enough to make him want to get home. Perhaps he would have to find another place—Bentwell's was getting rougher and less supervised.

As he left, he realized a lot of his clients were going to be disappointed. They would be facing another lonely night filled with the dread of dying, a night without the hope of being reborn in a young, healthy body.

A night without reconstruction.

3

Freddie Frank downed the last of his drink in one gulp. He had a baby face that made him look innocent, trustworthy, reliable—just the kind of person you would want to trust with your life if you were an angel. Many of his angels had, but had never been around to collect his money-back-guarantee. He was short and stocky, dressed in jodhpurs, riding boots, and pith helmet. He tapped his bare hairless chest with an antique riding crop.

"What else did he say?" he asked Mara.

"That's all, Freddie. I told you."

He suppressed the urge to break a few of her teeth. She was always lying to him, and he knew it. He leaned back in the form-fitting chair inside the private niche and smiled. Only on him it didn't quite look like a smile. He dropped his glass to get her attention. It shattered; the shards dissolved and were absorbed by the floor of Bentwell's.

"Tell me again," he demanded.

She sighed, then repeated what had happened with Dennis: what they had talked about, his refusal to hand over Warren, and his belligerent attitude. Freddie nodded, the entire situation at last understood.

Freddie and Dennis had been friends, once, but that had been a long time ago, before their careers had taken opposite swings, like the poles of a magnet. Friends. He was tired of being on the bottom, getting the dregs, the clients too far gone to attract anything but the most volatile angels, the angels who treated a procurer like slime.

What was wrong with his clients? They were people—real flesh and blood people, just like Dennis's clients. But, because of the way they looked or talked or acted, Freddie couldn't get as much money for them from an angel as he'd have liked.

Friends.

So a few angels had been killed while inside the white rooms at the Center. Could Freddie have stopped that? What was he supposed to do, stand there and watch every setup? Make sure the clients were on the receiving end all the time? Those angels who died could have been masos, for all anyone knew. Maybe killing the other person while having sex just wasn't kinky enough for them. Maybe the only way they could get off was by doing themselves in, too.

That was fine with Freddie.

But it was certainly no reason for Dennis Lange to be obsessed with pushing Freddie out of the business. He shook his head.

"Do you think he's ever going to go for a deal?" he asked Mara.

She looked amused by his question. "Why should he? He's set. He gets the best angels and the best clients. Why would he want to throw in with us?"

Freddie sighed as he realized the gravity of their situation. If he didn't do something soon, Dennis would absorb all of Freddie's angels and clients, and

leave him with nothing. He was untrained and un-
skilled in any other profession; finding another job
would take years. And over those years he would lose
everything he had. Everything. Including his crystal.

"We've got to do something, Mara. If it keeps up
like this, we'll be out of business in a month."

"That's not my fault, baby," she said.

He gritted his teeth and clenched his fists. "Did I
say it was?"

She shrugged.

The door to the niche was open, letting in the
sounds of the cleanup crew and the few people who
had no other place to go. They would walk out into
the dawn, another day of boredom, a day of sleep and
wasted time.

"All Dennis has to do is sit back and watch us go
under," Freddie moaned. "You're right. He'd never go
for a deal with us. Even *I* wouldn't consider a deal
with us."

Mara leaned forward and placed her hands on
Freddie's knees. "You know, Freddie, there *is* something we could do."

"Oh?"

"I have an ex-husband, from my last life. We
parted on good terms and I'm sure he'd see me if I
called him."

"Oh?"

She nodded. "Henri works for the Complex now.
You know how the Complex and the Centers don't get
along. Maybe he'd help us."

Freddie considered it. The Centers were private-
ly owned medical institutions which sold and financed
the life-crystals and provided the reconstruction process. They charged exorbitant rates and were a mo-
nopoly, overseen by the government's Complex. The
Complex recorded every reconstruction, amended the
tax records, kept track of births and deaths and recon-

structions, and watched carefully for illegal practices. With Henri's position in the Complex, he and Mara certainly had someone in the correct location. But would Henri actually do anything to help?

"Maybe." Freddie closed his eyes and tried to relax. The constant pressure of dealing with Dennis was getting to him, wearing him down. If something were to be done, it would have to be done soon. "All right. Talk to Henri. See what he can do."

She smiled and nodded. "No problem. I'm sure he'll—"

"Hello?"

They turned and looked through the doorway. Oleo Johnson stood there, bent over, so his head was visible.

"I didn't meant to interrupt, but I guess you're the only procurers left."

Freddie stood. "Come in."

They introduced themselves as Johnson entered. Freddie's head reached the middle of his chest. The ceiling in the niche was too low for Johnson, so he had to crouch. Freddie saw immediately that Johnson was not his normal type of angel; he was well-dressed, clean, and not abusive.

"I was wondering if you had anyone cancel. I'm looking for an interlude, and the sooner I get it, the better."

Freddie shook his head. "Sorry. No cancellations, but we do have a fifteen-year-old dust addict left."

Oleo made a face. "I was hoping for a woman."

"She *is* a woman," Freddie said. He glanced at his watch. "It's late, though. Too late to set it up for this morning. How about later on in the day? Do you work?"

Oleo nodded.

"How about after work, then?"

Oleo sighed. It wasn't exactly what he wanted, but it would have to do. At least it would be a woman, and she would be young. "That sounds nice. Very nice."

"Good. Let's take care of some of the details, then, shall we?" Mara asked.

4

There was no need for Dennis to bother with the manual controls, no need to see where they were going or where they had been, no feelings of discomfort making him wish the ride was over. The car's interior was like a small living room, with three low plush chairs and a very low short couch positioned around a coffee table. The wet bar behind him was filled with the drinks and drugs his angels liked. The walls were paneled, adding to the quiet mood of the dim lighting. It was close to five A.M.

Kira sat beside him, giggling, not bothering to try to control herself as Dennis had requested.

"I don't think I should take you to Bentwell's any more," he said.

She stopped swaying suddenly, as if he'd told her she was his next client. "What?"

"Take one of these," he said, holding out a small capsule. She wrinkled her face in an exaggerated expression of disgust. "I said, take one."

"You're no fun anymore," she said. She snatched the capsule from his palm and snapped it open under

18

her nose. Most of the vapor escaped but she inhaled enough to sober a little. "Now, what are you talking about?" she demanded.

"I just don't think it's a good idea for you to hang around Bentwell's anymore. At least not while I'm working."

"You're sick, Dennis, you know that? The guy didn't mean a thing to me. He never even touched me."

He smiled. "It doesn't have a thing to do with anyone you may have been with."

"Then what does it have to do with?" she asked.

He leaned back in his chair and crossed his legs. He liked to keep her as far out of his business as possible. She was so set against procuring, she'd use the incident with Mara to demand he leave the business. The implied threat of involving Kira had been strong—stronger than anything else the Franks had tried, and he didn't like that. He wanted Kira safely out of the way until he found out what was going on. If anything was going on at all.

"Tell me what you thought you were doing tonight," he said.

"What, at Bentwell's?"

He nodded. "Specifically with that angel. Howard Warren."

"Who?"

"Jesus. You don't even remember him. The lanky guy with the wavy hair and the thin mustache. The nervous one."

"That creep?"

"Yes, that creep."

She shook her head, smiling. "Did you see the way he was dressed? He was years out of touch with what's going on. Decades."

"He would have been good for a one-shot deal. Why did you say those things to him?"

"What did I say?" she asked.

"You don't remember?"

"Should I? All I remember is trying to fight off that fat bastard, Bentwell." She shuddered.

The car stopped; a relay clicked and the roof slid back. The doors opened downward to form exit ramps, and Dennis walked down and into the garage. The night air was cool and crisp but filled with the cloying scent of too-sweet flowers in bloom.

"What did I say to that perverted creep?" she shouted after him. "Dennis?"

He stopped in the driveway. "Come on. We'll go inside and I'll tell you." He waited for her to catch up, then took her arm as they walked up the driveway together. She walked out of synch with his steps, not moving closer to increase their contact, not moving far enough away to draw attention to her discomfort.

It was a sprawling ranch house in an exclusive neighborhood, with lots of tinted glass and gleaming steel. It looked solid and too heavy in the waning moonlight. The winding path went over a manicured lawn, up two steps, then stopped at a porch. Kira pressed her thumb to the doorlock and didn't wait for the automatic circuits; she slid it open manually.

The lights had already clicked on. They walked into the living room and sat on the couch.

"Well?" she asked. "What did I say?"

He looked at her, trying to decide if she really wanted to know. Her face was blank, slack, devoid of emotion, but that could have been from the long, tiring night.

"Listen, honey, some of these angels get off on being told how sick they are, how rotten and mean and ugly they are. It gives them a real boost. But not all of them look at it that way."

She stared at the ceiling, shaking her head.

"You managed to make Warren feel uncomfortable," he said.

"Will you tell me what I said?"

"You asked him what his preference was. You know what I mean. You've used it on others."

She shook her head. "Knives? Machine guns? That one?"

He nodded.

She shrugged. "So what? We didn't need him, and he was a one-shot deal. You said so yourself."

"You're looking at it wrong. Just try to consider what would happen if this got around. My reputation would be worse than Frank's."

She yawned deliberately. "Your reputation. That's too bad, dear. I'd hate for something like that to happen." She yawned again, stretching, throwing her arms out to her sides, causing the thin, clinging material of her gown to outline her small, rounded breasts. She held that position for a moment, then let her arms fall. "I'm tired. Is there anything else, or are this morning's lectures over?"

"Get some sleep," he said.

She nodded and smiled, as if his statement had been made out of consideration, then stood slowly, smoothing the gown's material over her hips and thighs. Dennis watched her move across the room and down the hall until she was out of sight.

Kira. It hadn't always been like this. Their relationship had changed without warning, without reason. He knew it couldn't have been solely her fault. At least this discussion had stopped before exploding into one of their fights. He wished he didn't love her; it would have made things so much easier.

He sighed and rubbed his face with his hands. His face muscles were sore, dead tired from the strain of keeping a mask of receptiveness, friendliness, and quiet control for the potential angels. His stomach was upset, but he couldn't tell if that was from too much booze or too much hunger. He didn't want to follow her into the bedroom yet. There was no need to see her accusing face, her sharp green eyes that bore though the layer of lies, the barriers he had carefully constructed for himself. She was sober, but she was anything but sympathetic.

He got up and walked to his den. The walls were in shadow, and little shards of light glinted off the plastic cases on the shelves that lined the right wall. The rust-colored carpeting faded to black in the corners. Before him, a few meters away from the opposite wall, was a long, simple white desk. Behind it was a black, comfortable, overstuffed chair.

He moved over to the shelves and started looking at the sides of the plastic cases. It was too dark to read their labels, but Dennis knew which program card he wanted, and its exact position on the shelf. How many times had he slipped that very same card into the mechanism in the arm of the CNS chair? A hundred? A thousand?

He snapped open the case, removed the wafer-thin card, and slipped it into the CNS chair's mechanism. He knew what was waiting for him—he had done this too many times to feel surprise—yet his heart beat faster and he grew excited in anticipation. The card unlocked something inside him, some feeling that came to life screaming in joy and terror as soon as the start button was pressed.

He sat awkwardly, quickly brushing the start button as soon as he was positioned. His eyes were closed before the circuits were activated.

It was called a roller coaster. It was an amusement ride in an amusement park, a long-dead place for recreation, out of vogue for hundreds of years. Dennis sat in the small, uncomfortable, foul-smelling car and waited for the man in the antique clothes to press the long wooden lever forward.

He knew every millimeter of the ride by heart— every movement, vibration, sound, smell, and sight were waiting to be unlocked, to be triggered. Off in the distance, gay lights shimmered and children squealed in delight. He was alone in the first car. He could hear the excited chatter of the people in the other cars behind him.

The man threw the lever, and the car clanked forward up a long, steep grade. When the string of cars reached the top, and Dennis saw what was waiting for him, he forgot he was home, in his den, sitting in a CNS chair.

The car plunged downward, leaving Dennis's stomach at the top of the rise. He screamed along with the others in the cars, releasing and venting some of his excitement and fear.

The cars went around once, shooting into the short narrow straightaway where the ride started. The man running the ride was smiling, arms crossed tightly, straw boater angled down over his eyes. Dennis realized the man was going to let the cars go around again. He'd had enough. Once was enough. He wanted to leap from the car to the wooden platform, but the car had already started its climb up the first big hill.

Too late.

He braced himself for the first rushing plunge downward. And then he saw it, at the top of the next hill. The tracks were broken. Right where they curved.

It was too late to do anything but scream. He was thrown free, soaring through the air like a wingless bird. The ground rushed up to greet him.

5

Howard Warren tried to live in a world of his own device, a world that sparkled like a rare jewel. Bentwell's had been more than he'd imagined possible and made his world tangible, gave him a taste of what he strove for—but only a taste. His one meager experience served to whet his appetite more than any of his daydreams ever had.

The people at the private club had been dressed like those Warren had seen in the news on the holo-set, like the rich people he worked for, like all the rich people he loathed and loved. He'd worn his best suit, his newest suit, and still he'd spent the evening feeling so far out of touch with what was going on that he might have been better off at home, with Paula. But he was glad he had gone.

Edmund Krowe, the entertainer, was Warren's cousin, and had permanent membership to all the best clubs all over the world. Warren dropped hints for a while, then ended up begging his cousin for a membership card. He promised to use it sparingly and not to do anything which might reflect badly on his cousin.

The card had arrived in the evening mail. Warren had stared at it, disbelief on his face, uncomprehending, euphoric, until his wife broke the spell.

"You're really planning on going?" Paula had asked.

He nodded.

"Good. Fine someone there, go home with her, and leave me alone."

Warren had smiled at her. She was a plain-looking woman with a pasty complexion and doughy body, with hair somewhere between mousy brown and washed-out dirty blonde.

"I will," he'd said. "With great pleasure."

And he had tried. But with the way he had been dressed, totally intimidated by the super-smooth, the super-slick, no one but the procurers would talk to him. He had approached Frank first, but refused to finalize anything with him. Frank hadn't struck him as being reliable or discreet, and discretion was something Warren valued highly. He hadn't gotten much of a chance to talk to Dennis Lange, but he did have his card, and his number was on his card. . . .

But he couldn't call from work. All outgoing calls were monitored. Working in the Center had some distinct advantages, like not having to pay for Paula's crystal, and getting fifty percent off their reconstructions, but security was tight and his fellow workers were anything but liberal. It would have been all right for his boss to call Lange—it was almost expected of those in the high management positions. But not Warren.

If his fellow workers overheard the call they would ride him, torment him, drop not-so-subtle hints as to his abnormal behavior, his enlarged view of himself, his traveling on the wrong side of the street. They might even beat him up, Warren thought, imagining bruises on his cheeks, eyes swollen shut.

Too many of his fellow workers had friends and relatives who'd had to become clients for some procurer. They'd let themselves be sexually molested, brutally assaulted, then killed. It was a tough life: reconstruction was expensive; an angel paid well for his thrills.

Warren, like almost all of his fellow workers, was an optimist. He sank all his spare income into paying for and maintaining his crystal. The crystals needed sophisticated equipment to function properly—lasers, microprocessors, the frame and laser guidance systems—and ended up costing close to twice as much as an exclusive single-family house in an enclosed neighborhood. But it was worth the expense.

The Centers could build you a new body, mold one of the undistinguished clones it always had on supply. As long as the Center could get an undamaged DNA chain, it could mold the clone's phenotype so it would look exactly like you had at twenty-five. With just one microscopic DNA molecule the new body would be genitically altered, starting slowly then building rapidly in a chain reaction until it would be an exact genetic duplicate. But without a crystal, Warren knew, you yourself would die. Your personality would be no more than a memory in your survivors' minds. And in Warren's case, he wasn't sure he would even be remembered.

Especially by Paula.

He looked around the office and tried to fathom what went on inside his fellow workers. There were probably some who shared his dream but were so frightened and stifled by their own lives, their lack of status, they were afraid to admit it. How many people sat at their desks day after day, shuffling papers, preparing data for some computer, rising to their feet only to shuffle to lunch, then back to their desks, then home, only to dream of being on the other side for once, of being on the top?

Warren knew he was on volatile ground. The only person even slightly pleased with his attitude was Paula, and that was only because she knew he would eventually leave her alone. Anyone else who found out about his rich, dangerous tastes would be quick to condemn without waiting for an explanation.

"Problem?"

Supervisor. She walked up and down aisles between the endless rows of desks, making sure that work was being done, that no one slacked off. Warren licked his lips and tried to smile.

"No. I was working on a personal problem."

"You're docked fifteen minutes." She leaned over and noted the number on his desk, and Warren caught a brief hint of her musty perfume. "Personal problems on your own time."

The supervisor walked away without waiting for a response, an apology, or an explanation. She knew there would be none. One word from her and Warren would be out of a job. Money was tight, and jobs hard to find. The Center's Financing Department would close in; his and Paula's crystals would be wiped clean, then re-sold.

He looked down at the desktop. Large enough for two stacks of paper, some pencils, his hands, and an in-out tray. He shuffled the top piece of paper to the out tray without glancing at it, then read the paper beneath—a requisition for 17 tonnes of ball bearings. He sighed, thinking about what he would have liked to have done with those bearings, and what he wanted to do to Lange's good-looking but snotty wife.

6

"I can't believe he's a broker," Freddie Frank said.

"Look, we both checked him out. He's a broker. Let me get some sleep, will you?" Mara asked, rolling away from him.

The buoyant force beneath them shifted, readjusted to the new weight distribution, then settled down again. The warm night air moved slowly and gently over their bodies. Freddie put his hands behind his head and made faces at his reflection in the mirrored ceiling.

"You think he'll use us again? Maybe he thought we were the only ones left."

"Jesus, Freddie, will you stop? We *were* the only ones left. It's nine o'clock. The sun is up. We've got to get some rest, or we won't be able to do anything this evening. I need some sleep."

He touched her on the shoulder. "I tell you, Mara, I don't like him. I don't like anything about him."

She sighed and sat up in bed. "All right. Tell me."

"He gives me the creeps."

"He's an angel, Freddie. He's supposed to give you the creeps."

"When I checked him out I found out what his nickname is. You know what it is?"

She shook his head.

"Oleo. His nickname is Oleo. What the hell kind of a name is that for an investment broker?" he whined.

"Are you really worried?" Mara asked.

Freddie nodded. "I just can't afford to have anything go wrong. Lange is right on my ass, waiting for me to make a slip so he can push me out."

"Nothing's going to go wrong," she said, spreading her arms, inviting him closer. He bent over and gently began to suck on one of her nipples. It soothed him, took his mind off his problems. A soft matronly smile spread across her face; she did her best to ignore the tingling feeling spreading out through her chest. "Don't worry, Freddie. Nothing's going to go wrong," she cooed, rocking back and forth gently, his head cradled in her arms, clutched tightly to her chest.

"Nothing," Freddie murmured.

His troubles melted away. Lange, Johnson, Bentwell, Mara: they all dissolved into an eddy of nothingness and he fell asleep, as totally at peace as he had ever been.

When he awoke, Mara was gone. He stretched slowly, luxuriating in the well-rested feeling that suffused through his body. He got out of bed and padded across and into the bathroom, staring long and hard at his reflected image.

The stress of his job was starting to show. It had to be the stress—he wasn't old enough to start looking like this.

Each afternoon, when he awoke, he would try to ignore the wrinkles and creases around his eyes and the corners of his mouth. But they stayed until he finally had the makeup unit prepare him for the evening. It was something he didn't like to think about. He pulled his skin taut around his eyes to help the unit do its job. When it was done, he looked like the Freddie Frank his clients and angels had come to know, baby face and all.

He sighed, disgusted with the way his life was going, what his business had turned into. He had let Oleo Johnson get one of his best clients, that dust addict, without signing a confession. He had promised to sign it later, after he had killed her; but not before. Freddie swore at himself, letting himself be intimidated like that. And it was all Lange's fault. Lange had him running scared. Well, not for long, he thought.

Freddie had his usual breakfast: tuna fish, a short glass of vodka, three pieces of buttered toast, and half a kiwi fruit. He was dressed in his standard working outfit—riding jodhpurs, knee boots, pith helmet, and riding crop. Normally he wouldn't have bothered, but tonight he wore a polo shirt, complete with a tiny green crocodile patch sewn just above his left breast. He had never seen a real crocodile, though he had a vague idea as to what they were. What escaped him was why anyone would want one sewn onto their shirt. But it was the fashion, and Freddie knew better than to question fashion.

Mara Frank could have named a dozen places she would have rather been, but she needed Henri's help. He lived in the same sterile penthouse he had when they were married forty years ago, and, as she stepped out of the elevator tube, she saw he hadn't even redecorated.

Henri was two centimeters shorter than she, slim and athletic, a good-looking vital man. He walked with self-confidence in an easy-going stride, crossing the room to greet her at the tube. She noticed the touch of grey around his temples and thought it looked good, distinguished.

"It's good to see you again."

He slipped his arms around her waist and kissed her cheek. "It's good to see *you*," he said. "But come in, come in. We've got a lot to catch up on. How long has it been?"

"Too long, Henri. Too long."

They walked down the short entrance hall and entered the living room. It was larger than she remembered. The couches, chairs, lamps, and tables were all suspensor units, furniture without legs, arms, cushions, or support poles, floating in a buoyant field. Colorful fabrics and rich tapestries outlined the important parts of the furniture, providing the idea of where to sit. Henri led her to the couch, and they sat.

"So, Mara. What's wrong? Tell me."

"Wrong? What makes you think something's wrong?"

He chuckled lightly, and the little laugh sounded pleasant and sweet, like a crystal-clear spring rushing over smooth rocks. "We're not one-timers, you know. We've both been around. One of my ex-wives calls me and says she'd like to see me, that it's important. A lot of years have passed, a lot of people, a lot of problems. Now, tell me what it is."

He was so tender, so caring, so real, she knew she had him right there. Comparing him with Freddie would help bring on the necessary tears, the small force which would push Henri over to help her.

"I've got to go, Henri. I can't stay. I'm sorry." She fought back the tears, now, knowing that it would increase their effect when they came.

"No. You're not going. Not yet. Not until I find out what's bothering you." He held her hands. They were trembling, and he squeezed them lightly, hoping to reassure her. "You're what, thirty this time? Five years into this new life? A whole other life between

31

me and him? How long have you been with Freddie?"

She started crying. She hoped she had timed it right. He held her tightly and rocked her from side to side, comforting her. She thought about Freddie, how differently he would have reacted to tears, how differently he would have treated her.

She wished Freddie had some of Henri's charm. It would have made things so much simpler. But she was the one who had found Freddie, had known what he was like all along, had known his limitations, both intellectually and emotionally; she'd been aware of all this before they married. Freddie needed her. He was counting on her to come through.

Lightly, she pushed herself away from Henri and, through her crying, managed to ask for a drink. He got up to get her one. She used the time and distance to maintain her cold, hard frame of mind, to set Henri up for the rest. She pushed her long black hair behind her shoulders.

Henri returned and handed her a glass. She accepted it gladly, holding it as though it were a prop, something to sip at during the silences.

"What was it like for you? Your last life?" he asked when she had stopped crying completely.

She thought back: first Henri, a reconstruction, then a series of short affairs, hooking up with that embezzler, talking him into going for a reconstruction for her, promising him at least a part of her next life, this life, and then meeting Freddie Frank.

"Dull," she said. "But better than the alternative."

Henri smiled. "Yes. It would be."

She took a sip of her drink, then launched into a careful explanation of the situation at Bentwell's, and about Freddie. Henri made her stop and explain some of the actions that had taken place. He'd never had the urge to use a procurer, although he could certainly afford their fees. He seemed genuinely fascinated by the details of the process—more so than he was by either Freddie or Dennis. But by the time she was finished she had made her point, and he understood the type of help she wanted and needed.

He shook his head. "No way. It can't be done. It could start a war between the Centers and the Complex. I cannot and will not officially act in any way on something like this."

Mara felt something inside tighten, constrict around her stomach like a shrinking band of metal. "Freddie and I are going to do something. We have to. Whether you help us or not."

He shook his head. "No way. Not with my help. This thing is like a gang war, Mara. Lange has a lot of friends. Some of his angels are people in very high positions. If I committed the Complex and all of its administrative functions toward destroying Lange— no. There's nothing I can do. Officially."

"I understand, Henri. I really do. But there must be *some*thing you could do to help," she said, knowing she had him.

He sighed and rubbed his eyes. "Yes, I suppose there is. I suppose there is. There's always something that can be done. Someone's always doing it."

Mara smiled and put her hand on his shoulder. "Let's have dinner and discuss some of the details, then, shall we?"

Freddie sat in a chair in his living room, slapping his palm with the riding crop. Each time it struck, it stung, and a sharp sound bounced off the walls. He was waiting for Mara.

If she didn't arrive soon, they'd be late for Bentwell's. And if they were late, they'd have to sit on the outskirts of the crowd, or in one of the small lounges, too far removed from where the real action took place. The other procurers would have staked out their territories and left him with the dregs again.

He liked Bentwell's. His luck there was better than it had ever been at any other club. Just by being there when all the other procurers had left had gotten him an angel. That Oleo Johnson.

He glanced at the clock on the coffee table. If Mara didn't arrive soon, he would have to leave without her. Johnson would probably be getting ready to do in his victim pretty soon—the small white room at the Center had been reserved for eleven.

If anything went wrong with Johnson—no, nothing was going to go wrong, he told himself. But still, if it did, it would be all over, and Freddie knew it. He would be out of business, out of money, faster than any way possible. He'd have to move out of the less-than-expensive house he barely maintained, and giving that up would only be the beginning. Mara would leave him; he would have to undergo force-training to learn an entirely new profession, only he didn't have the money for that; his crystal would be taken back to the Center and wiped clean; his own chances at being reconstructed would be slim; and he might even have to spend some time in one of the retraining institutions. He would be a one-timer. A one-timer.

And all because of a broker, an angel named Oleo Johnson.

If Johnson screwed up at all, if anything went wrong, the police would be called in and an investigation would be made. Freddie would be ruined. Why hadn't he insisted that Johnson sign that confession last night, when he should have?

Freddie nodded and slapped his palm again. He knew why. If he'd insisted that Johnson sign it then, there would have been a better than even chance of Johnson waiting, then taking his business elsewhere. And Freddie couldn't afford to have that happen. He needed every angel—he didn't have Lange's reputation or clients, and he couldn't charge the fees that bastard could. How the hell did Lange get away with it?

He glanced at the clock again.

The door opened and Mara waltzed in, looking

like she had fallen in love for the first time. She had a lot of nerve coming in this late, smiling like a damned fool.

"Hi, Freddie. Put a smile on your face," she said, crossing the room.

He slapped his palm with some force. "Smile, huh? Smile?" He leapt to his feet and took two quick steps toward her, then swung the riding crop at her side. An angry red line appeared on her thigh.

"Take it easy! Hey!"

He hit her harder. "Smile? Where the hell have you been? You know what time it is?"

He moved to strike her again, but Mara grabbed the crop and ripped it out of his hand. Her mouth hardened and her eyes narrowed. She waved the crop at him while rubbing the welts on her leg. "Sit," she said.

He sat. He was taken aback, never having seen this side of Mara before.

"I'm not even sure I should tell you, now," she said, towering over him, hands on hips.

"You're a goddamned waste, Mara. You know that? That riding crop doesn't scare me. Now, you were late, and you're going to tell me why you were late. And if the reason you give me isn't good enough, I'll beat the shit out of you. And if you don't tell me, I'll still beat the shit out of you. Now tell me."

She sat opposite him, dropping the riding crop to the table as though it were poisoned. "I was having dinner with Henri."

"Henri?"

She nodded.

"Well? Did you talk to him? Will he help?"

She nodded and a little smile crept to her lips. "He'll help, all right, but not in exactly the way we wanted. But with a little work on our part, and a little help from him, we should be able to get rid of Lange. For good."

"What?"

She sighed. "Lange's a pain in the ass, isn't he?"

"Yeah."

"Well, with him gone, all of his clients and angels are going to have to find someone else to handle them. . . ."

"Yeah," he said, leaning over, smiling. "And they'd be waiting for just the right person to come along—just the right kind of procurer."

She nodded. "And Henri's willing to help."

He looked at her smile and, suddenly, didn't like it. "For old time's sake, I suppose."

7

"Hi. How are you?" Dennis asked the slim, pale girl with sunken eyes and high cheekbones.

"I could be better," she said.

Dennis smiled and shifted his drink to his left hand. She couldn't have been more than fifteen and she'd already used Dennis's services twice. She had an allowance nearly as large as Dennis's income, and was spoiled to the point of not knowing that life could be any different. Her parents had no idea as to how much money they actually had, but Dennis did; they had bought stock in the Reconstruction Centers right before they'd burst into economic and social dominance.

Bentwell's was better this night, and Dennis was almost enjoying himself, not thinking about business too much, not having to worry about where Kira was, what she was doing.

"My parents found out," the girl said.

"What happened?" Dennis asked cautiously.

"They tried to make me think I was sick at first, that I needed help." She shrugged. "I wasn't going to argue with them about that—not when I knew all about them. I wonder where the hell they thought I got your number, or the invitation to Bentwell's. They're such hypocrites."

He laughed. "Did you tell them you knew?"

"About them?"

He nodded.

"I sure as hell did," she said, smiling. "I had to so they would lighten up. You should have seen their faces, though. They turned three shades of red. They looked at each other, and then I realized that he had never really known about her using your services, and that she hadn't known about him using you. It was very interesting."

"I bet."

"They both tried to deny the whole thing, put up a glorious front for their little girl, but that didn't work. Then they tried to throw the whole thing back at me, like it was my fault, but when I told them where I found your cards they knew I had to be telling the truth. Quite a scene."

"As long as no harm was done," Dennis said.

"No, no harm. They just cut off my allowance for a little while, those lovable pieces of shit."

He smiled. "It's not really that bad—it'll be over before you know it. Just try to think of it as a temporary inconvenience."

"That's easy for you to say."

Dennis smiled and shrugged. They drifted away from each other, through the silent, invisible understanding that cocktail parties bring on. He walked around the main lounge, looking for the right group of people to spend some time with. Every group he wandered near was talking about something he either knew nothing about or knew too well. Dennis caught snatches of conversations about art, the CNS chairs, and unsolved murders, and continued to look for the right group to fit his mood.

He finished the drink, placed it on the suspensor table floating about waist height, and decided to check out the dance room. He left the lounge and followed the familiar signs to the entrance tube.

Through the round doorway, a line of chairs sat on the floor; the whirling, blurred dance room was beyond. Getting to the dance floor by foot was impossible, and there were signs placed all around to caution anyone from trying. Dennis ignored the signs— he'd traversed the tube too many times while drunk or stoned or tripping; the few drinks he'd had weren't going to affect him.

Five meters into the tube was the first chair. He knew he should sit down and let the chair transport him the length of the tube to the dance floor, but he had never taken the first chair, and wasn't about to start now. The next chair was a few meters beyond, right where the floor in the tube started to move. It was difficult to maintain footing there, but he had done it before. He liked to think of it as a challenge. He had to adopt a side-step just to remain on his feet. He had managed to reach the third chair only once, and that was only because Kira had goaded him while he had been too drunk to realize the risk.

The third chair was a meter beyond the point where the tube spun so fast it was necessary to run at top speed to avoid being thrown down and pinned to the tube. Forward movement was difficult, requiring slow, steady progress. He leapt onto the rotating floor and started running for all he was worth. He got a hand on the back of the chair, still running at top speed, then managed to get his other hand on it, too. He jumped over the seat back and safely landed on the cushion. As soon as he was settled, the chair moved forward.

By the time the chair reached the end of the tube, centrifugal force had taken over. When he looked back he could tell he was spinning, but when he looked forward to the dance room everything looked normal enough.

He got out of the chair and stepped onto the tube's floor/walls/ceiling. He knew his head was somewhere near the center of the tube and that he was being spun over and over, but it didn't feel like it.

He walked onto the dance floor.

Three drunk couples were sitting on the ceiling, laughing and joking high over Dennis's head. Bentwell was lying on the wall to his right, a martini glass defying gravity by resting on his stomach, perpendicular to Dennis's sense of "up." He shook his head, forcing himself to readjust his way of thinking.

The room was spherical, and the only entrance or exit was through the tube. Lights flashed on and off at random, adding to his sense of disorientation. There was no music, though; dancing was an activity that flitted in and out of vogue too quickly to be anticipated. Tonight, dancing was definitely out.

Bentwell looked ridiculous in his flowing shocking-pink toga and matching football cleats, lying on the floor like that. Dennis moved to his right, toward Bentwell and, as he walked, the couples on the ceiling seemed to move closer until they appeared to be sittting on the wall.

"Pete?"

The middle-aged man stirred, then looked up. He placed his drink on the floor and sat up. "Hello, Dennis." He rubbed his eyes. "How's business?"

"Not bad," Dennis said, sitting down next to him. "And yours?"

Bentwell grimaced. "It would be one hell of a lot better if I had less second-rate procurers like Freddie Frank coming around."

"What's wrong? Something happen?"

"He tried to stiff me last night."

"He got an angel?"

Bentwell nodded. "Oleo Johnson. Got him right before we closed, and even though two of my floor managers saw them shake hands, and overheard the deal being consummated, he *still* tried to stiff me. He knows that those booths have recorders going in them."

Dennis laughed. "I wouldn't worry too much about Freddie. He's a nice enough guy." He took a sip from his drink. "We used to be pretty close, Freddie and I. That was before he got mixed up with Mara, though. Before his luck started turning sour. We'd even talked about becoming partners at one point."

Bentwell raised his eyebrows and opened his eyes wide in disbelief. "Partners? With Frank?"

Dennis nodded. "Sure, but that was a long time ago. I still think he's basically a good person, Pete. He's just been getting some bad breaks. You'll see. He'll straighten out once things start going his way. Right now, he's so busy spending all of his time fighting a bad reputation that he's been forced to become somewhat of an opportunist."

"That's a hell of a nice way to put it," Bentwell said.

Dennis shrugged. "He'll come across with your percentage. And don't worry—if he doesn't, I'll cover for him. Locking him out of your place isn't what he needs."

Bentwell grunted. "I hope you're right."

Dennis took another sip, savoring the scotch's sour taste. "So do I, Pete. So do I. Let's give him some time to straighten out, though, okay?"

"Well, he's got—" he checked his watch dangling from a gold chain around his neck "—seven hours to come up with the money. Twenty-four hours after the deal was made."

Dennis shrugged. "Like I said. If he doesn't come across, let me know and I'll make good for him."

Bentwell shook his head. "It's your money, pal. What you do with it's no concern of mine. As long as I get what's due, then I don't care who pays."

"That's what I like about you, Peter. You always do the right thing. And it always comes from the heart."

Someone else had entered the dance room. Bentwell was looking at her, trying to place the plain, nondescript face. Dennis looked over and recognized her immediately.

"Know her?" Bentwell asked.

Dennis nodded. "An angel, believe it or not. Mary White. You've heard of her parents—also angels of mine. Bill and Rose White."

"She's looking at us."

"I know. Do me a favor, Pete? If she takes even one step toward us, take off. I talked with her earlier and I have a feeling that she's got something she wants to tell me."

"Right," Bentwell said. He got up and walked around in a small circle, stretching his pudgy legs. "I think I'll get a fresh drink anyway. I could use one."

"Fine." Bentwell left the room and the girl walked around looking over her head, behind her, trying to get a perspective on her surroundings. Dennis sat and waited. She walked slowly, casually, as if sightseeing in a museum, until she was by Dennis's side. He put on his smooth smile.

"Sit?" he asked.

She started, then looked down. "Oh, it's you," she said in mock surprise. "I didn't see you." She sat. "I'm glad we kind of bumped into each other, though. I remembered something I wanted to talk to you about."

Dennis smiled. "Oh?"

"Well, I guess I was sort of looking for you."

"I thought so. What's wrong?"

"I already told you about what my parents did when they found out what happened, didn't I? About their cutting off my allowance?"

"Yes, you did."

"Well, I need money."

"Oh?"

She nodded. "After tonight, I'll be broke."

Dennis shook his head. "That's too bad, Mary. I wish there was something I could do, but you know how things are. I can't loan money."

"Yeah, but—"

"No. I can't loan money. It's the law. Even if I wanted to and could afford to, I couldn't. They'd have my license in no time at all."

She licked her lips and continued to stare straight at the floor. He didn't like the strain he saw in her profile; her cheek muscles were tense, accentuating her high cheekbones, and her jaw muscles were drawn, giving her head the appearance of an animate skull.

"Well, what about . . . what about taking me on?" she asked, quickly looking into his eyes with two burning embers.

She was serious. Her eyes were black holes imploring him, pulling him closer and closer to where she wanted him. Dennis wasn't sure he wanted to deal with her desperate plea; she was very young, and her parents were very influential.

"You don't need the money that badly," Dennis said flatly, hoping to put an end to the conversation.

"But I do," Mary said. "There are . . . other considerations."

"Then borrow the money from your parents."

She shook her head. "They refuse to even discuss money with me. I can't borrow from a bank, and I've got no personal credit. Now, will you take me on?"

Mary White. Interesting, but dangerous. Very dangerous, he thought. Somewhere between thirteen and fifteen, relatively attractive in a moribund sense, daughter of a man who has more money than he could spend in fifty lifetimes. A man who could crush Dennis without a second thought if he found out. A man who lived and breathed trouble. Lots of trouble. The kind of trouble Dennis knew he couldn't get out of with any amount of talk, influence, or money.

"How old are you, Mary?"

"Sixteen."

"Can you prove it?"

She handed him her ID. He looked it over carefully and checked for signs of tampering or falsification. If it had been altered, it had been a professional job and was too good for Dennis to detect. He shrugged and handed it back to her.

"I don't think it's a good idea, Mary. I really don't. You're not the average type of client. Most of the time, all the client gets out of being sexually abused, then murdered, and not necessarily in that order, is a free trip to the Center. The angel covers the cost of the victim's reconstruction, pays my fee, and then I have to give a percentage of my fee to Bentwell, or whoever owns the place where I made the contact or deal—"

"Then you won't do it."

"I didn't say that. I was just trying to tell you that under normal conditions, the client gets nothing. Except reconstruction. How much money do you need?"

She bit her lip as if trying to decide if she should hit him high or tell him the exact amount. "Seventy-five thousand."

He nodded. Not too bad. It was possible . . . if he found the right angel. But that would take time, and he wasn't sure how long Mary was willing to wait. "It can be done," he said slowly, evenly, trying not to get her hopes up. "All it'll take is time. I'll just have to find the right angel. You wouldn't want to walk into one of those pretty white one-way rooms with a butcher, now, would you?"

She shook her head.

The longer she thought it would take, the better, Dennis thought. There was a chance she would back out, and that was by all means better than taking that kind of chance with her father.

"Like I said, it's going to take time to find the

right person. Your name carries a lot of weight in most circles, you know."

"Then you'll do it?"

He nodded. "Sure. I don't trust anyone else to handle it properly." He smiled and put a friendly arm around her bony shoulder. It dug into his forearm. "If you get any second thoughts, let me know. We can call this off any time until I find us an angel."

She smiled and nodded. "Okay. And Dennis?"

"Yes?"

"Thanks."

8

Oleo had time to go home and change after work. He needed a shower, a shave, and a few hours sleep. He even had time to browse through his den to make sure the glove was the weapon he wanted to use. When he had taken care of all he could, he lay down on his suspensor bed and tried to get some rest.

He closed his heavy-lidded eyes and rolled onto his side, thinking about the fifteen-year-old dust addict he was going to take care of in a few hours. He wondered what she looked like, what kind of person she was, what made her turn to drugs at all, and if she would enjoy what Oleo had planned for her. He knew she came from one of the slums, from one of the sections where murder was a fair exchange for a loaf of bread, where murder lacked its finesse, charm, and excitement. But then, for all its bad points, murder was free in the slums.

If only he'd read the fiche on Berkoff.

Berkoff.

And Oleo was wide awake, sitting up, trying to figure out what had gone wrong at the office. Perhaps he should call Frank, cancel out for the evening—

thinking about Berkoff would ruin his fun, break his train of concentration. It had been a grandly stupid thing to do, Oleo thought.

He had arrived at the office late, strung out, his entire body feeling like a rubber band stretched too tight. His eyes had been gritty, his mouth had tasted foul, and he'd been tired. He'd had no patience for anything. The stimulants had helped, but irritability was one of their side effects, which came to the surface soon after Oleo had settled into his chair.

Berkoff had been waiting for him in the outer office. His secretary had given him the ultrafiche file on Berkoff, and foolishly, Oleo hadn't read it. He hadn't thought it was needed, and there hadn't been the time.

He'd shown Berkoff some of the standard investments, and Berkoff had reacted violently.

"Enough!" Berkoff had spat, cutting off Oleo's description of a solid company that was looking for investors.

"Is something wrong?" Oleo had asked.

"No, nothing is wrong, Mr. Johnson. It is simply a matter of understanding. You are showing me what you feel are fine, solid investments. I do not share your opinion."

That's direct enough, Oleo had thought. "What did you have in mind, then?"

Berkoff's lips had stretched ever so slightly, widening his mouth into a thin, cruel smile. "Come now, Mr. Johnson. Evidentally you haven't done your research."

Oleo had looked confused.

"Do you know who I represent? Have you any idea as to how much money I have to invest?"

Oleo had shrugged. "Not really."

"Very well, then. Good day." Berkoff had risen to his feet and walked to the door.

"Hey, wait a minute," Oleo had said, quickly following Berkoff to the door. "Have a little understanding, will you? I didn't get any sleep and had to—"

"Good day," Berkoff had repeated.

Oleo remembered how the short balding man had walked out of the office, leaving him feeling worse than before. He'd had one of his men in the lobby of the building follow Berkoff. He'd checked his ultrafiche file and seen the amount of capital Berkoff had available for investing, and almost cried. With that kind of money, investing in the Reconstruction Centers was possible, and to get any kind of toe-hold in that organization was akin to nothing else in the world.

And Oleo had let it all slip by.

He rolled over and pressed the red button by his phone. A few seconds later, a familiar voice, his secretary, said hello.

"Hello, Susan. Heard anything yet?" Oleo asked in the general direction of his nightstand.

"No, nothing. Berkoff still hasn't gone to another broker. He hasn't gone back to his hotel yet, either."

"All right. Is our man still with him?"

"Yes."

"Good. Let me know if anything happens."

"Yes, sir."

He pressed the disconnect button and lay back. Why hadn't Berkoff done as he'd threatened? Why hadn't he gone to another broker? Or, better yet, why hadn't he returned to his hotel? Oleo's man who was following Berkoff had reported that he had entered an old run-down building in the downtown area. A man with Berkoff's power and money had no reason to go down there, to the slums. No reason.

Not nice, Oleo thought. Not nice at all.

It didn't make sense. The man had put on a big show of being insulted, had pushed his way by Oleo and out of the office, and had threatened to see another broker immediately. But maybe he couldn't do it that easily—maybe he had to get approval before shifting to another broker. Perhaps there was still time to get him back before his superiors okayed the switch.

But if that were true, and Johnson still had a chance to get Berkoff's business, then what the hell was he doing in a slum building?

No, Oleo thought. Not nice at all.

To hell with him. An evening filled with charm, excitement, and fun lay ahead, just waiting for Oleo, and he wasn't about to let this short European man spoil it for him. He glanced at his glove sitting on the nightstand and smiled. He closed his eyes, hoping to get a little rest, to take the edge off his raw nerves before going to the Center.

Oleo looked through the room's transparent wall from one of the private viewing booths outside the small white room. She was already inside, waiting, a dull, bored, unaware look in her glassy eyes. Since he was the angel, he was entitled to use one of the booths to prepare himself. He wondered how many other booths were taken. The Centers used good business sense and sold voyeurs the right to view the sexual interaction from a private, confidential booth. All for a healthy price, of course. Oleo didn't think all the booths were occupied, though, since it had been Frank's setup.

He checked to make sure his hood was in the right position. It was black, with eye and mouth holes cut out, and was required by law. In Oleo's case, the hood was worthless; anyone wanting to know his identity could easily find it out, thanks to his height.

He stood, slipped the glove onto his right hand, and left the booth. He stood before the room's clear wall for a moment, watching the girl's discomfort.

She had probably been pretty at one time, before the dust had gotten to her. Oleo was glad that Frank had told him her age; he would have found it difficult to believe by looking at her. Her face alone made her look fifty. There were lines, deep lines, etched in her face—lines of worry and horror around her eyes and mouth, like she had seen and done too much in her short life. Oleo thought the lines and creases were most probably from the dust.

Her eyes showed awareness every few seconds as if her mind was wandering through fantasy and reality at an incredible rate and happened to hit upon the reality of the moment. She knew what was going to happen and Oleo saw that she knew; her eyes were cold, hard, empty.

Oleo smiled. He liked her.

Nice. Nice indeed.

He opened the door and stepped into the antiseptic-smelling room. She jumped to her feet when he entered. She stood awkwardly, unsure of what was expected of her, looking around the room, letting her gaze settle on everything but Oleo. The sound of the door clicking shut startled them both.

"Hello," Oeo said, smiling beneath his hood.

She said nothing. Oleo got angry.

He leapt forward and, with the speed of a rattler, struck the upper fleshy part of her arm with his right, gloved hand. For an instant, nothing happened. Then the pain of the glove's contact made itself known; that area of her arm quickly became a red pulp of bleeding flesh.

The blood didn't flow quickly—Oleo knew what he was doing. The blow had been meant to shake her up, not to do real damage. After all, it was early, and the room was booked for enough time to let him do whatever he liked at whatever pace he chose.

She was staring at her arm, disbelief stamped on her face.

"I said, hello," Oleo said.

She looked at him. "Hello," she said emotionlessly.

"There, now. That's better, isn't it? Why don't you sit down and relax?" he asked.

She sat on the edge of the bed. It was old and stained, a solid mattress and boxspring. He didn't mind; he knew what a lot of blood could do to a suspensor bed's mechanism.

She was clutching her arm, trying to stem the flow of blood.

He smiled as he felt himself grow excited. He advanced and sat on the bed beside her. His tall frame made her seem tiny and he savored that thought, thinking of her as a child, with him as her punishing father.

He grabbed a handful of material at her neck and yanked downward with all his might. The dress separated along its seams, exposing her breasts. She didn't move. Her chest raised and lowered with each breath, her lips moving to a silent prayer.

Oleo leaned over and cupped her right breast in his right hand. He kept his touch very light but the needles still did their work, puncturing the fleshy underside of her breast. He waited a moment until the blood started to flow and collect in his palm, then bent over and lifted his hood a little with his left hand.

His mouth was free.

He licked his lips, then bit down hard and savagely on her right nipple. She screamed and jerked away, crawled into the corner like a panicked animal in the middle of a forest fire.

He watched her, savoring her fear.

She was becoming a solid mass of crimson flesh.

Nice, Oleo thought. Very nice indeed.

She cried, screamed, sobbed, babbled hysterically, thrashed about on the bed, then finally, turning away from him, tried to find a way through the clean white walls with her fingernails.

Oleo was ready.

He removed his jump suit slowly, enjoying the tortured whimpering animal noises escaping her lips. He stood beside the bed admiring his handiwork, then bent down to straddle her shoulders and pin her down.

She glared at him, her eyes now deeply embedded in the reality of the moment, insane with animal fear, pain, and hate, then sat up quickly and ripped the hood from his head before he realized what she was going to do.

He slapped her in the face with his right, gloved hand. Only one other person had ever done that to him, a girl too long dead and reborn to remember.

This was it. He had to work fast.

He rammed into her.

9

She was married to him, but did that mean she had to do whatever he said, react like a trained dog? Stay home, he'd said. Do something domestic, he'd said. Watch a few programs in the holoroom, find a good program for the CNS chair, keep out of trouble, and I'll be home soon, he'd said.

She'd stifled her anger, her frustration, the turmoil she felt every time Dennis treated her like that, every time he left her home alone, and had smiled. Kira had plenty of opportunities to learn his smile and to practice it on him.

When they'd first been married things had been different. They'd had a lot of fun on their honeymoon, sharing private jokes, making fun of the people around them, spending money, trying to impress people who couldn't be impressed by their display. They drank hard, played hard, and took in all the sights the little resort town had to offer. When they were done, they left behind the town and hotel as if they were empty shells inhabited by ghosts.

But then, Dennis hadn't become a procurer yet.

They returned to the city, moving into the apartment they'd both carefully selected to share their life together, before she realized the honeymoon was over.

Kira shook her head and took another sip of mescanol. No. None of that was true. It hadn't happened that way at all. Well, that wasn't exactly true, either. Some of it had happened, but she knew it wasn't the fairy-tale beginning she liked to tell herself it was. They had their problems even back then. But not on the honeymoon. No, not the honeymoon. That had been just as she remembered.

She placed the glass on the table before her and looked around the living room. It was a little frightening for her to actually acknowledge how and where she was living. She remembered her parents' house, a small four-room condominium on the outskirts of New York, and how crowded the five of them had been. Her two brothers had had to double up in a bedroom; that alone wouldn't have been that bad, but the paper-thin walls, the smallness of each and every one of those four rooms, the smell in the kitchen her mother could never get rid of, her embarrassment when a man picked her up at the house, the things she heard through her brothers' adjoining bedroom walls, the times someone walked in on her while she was in the bathroom, all added up to make the house a lethal claustrophobic trap.

One room had to serve as the kitchen, dining room, holoroom, den, and living room. The room was in constant use, each member of the family wanting to do something else, talk about something else, watch something else on the holo, entertain someone else— the anxiety of sharing the room made them a quiet, bored family, ready to explode. It was a small, cramped home.

Kira looked at the painting on the opposite wall. It was ten meters long and three meters high, a ridiculously large painting that neither she nor Dennis liked. Dennis had paid more for it than her father had paid for his whole condo. The couch she sat on cost more than all the furniture her parents had ever bought. The dress she wore cost more than all the clothes her parents had bought for her over ten years.

She was thirty-one, extremely attractive, and very bored. Bored and frustrated. She hated to stay in the house by herself, and yet she didn't want to work. It was a big house, too big for two people, and the walls made noises and the floor creaked. Every week she had to walk through each of the rooms to update whatever was inside them, keep up on what was new, what pieces of furniture were still stylish, which ones had to be replaced, the latest suspensor units, the newest designer bric-a-brac, the newest piece of sculpture by what's his name, the most expensive "living" carpeting, the subtle automatic lighting systems. . . .

The honeymoon had been ideal. Even their first apartment had been good. But this house was bad.

She knew better than to blame her discontent on the house, though. She knew the difference between a house and a home. And she had a very good idea what was gnawing away at her ego, her sense of being worth something as a person. She knew what made her depressed, what made her give Dennis an impossible time when she really wanted to be loving and understanding.

He was a procurer.

And that was enough.

She picked up her glass and flung it at the painting. It smashed against the canvas and dripped the best mescanol money could buy down its surreal surface. She felt no better, and the painting was still hanging, still making her face it, stare at it, look at its ridiculous colors and shapes.

Dennis. A procurer.

She told herself it was just a high-paying job, one that required meeting people and helping them out, that it was an important part of the reconstruction process, that procurers were needed by society. Maybe it would have been different if she hadn't talked Dennis into taking her along to a Center so she could see one of his angels in action. Maybe. But it was too late to change that.

She spun around and struck a floating lamp with her fist. It shattered; the larger pieces, still caught in the suspensor field, floated at the same height, while tiny shards and slivers, too small for the field to buoy up, floated to the floor like powdered, glittering rain. The room was dimmer, the walls a step closer.

The phone rang.

She clenched her fists and screamed, screamed with all the power, all the hostility, and all the terror she had been denying herself all evening.

The phone rang.

She strode across the carpet, its cushioned surface and texture giving her step a bounce she didn't want, and stopped before the doorway to Dennis's den.

The phone rang.

She crossed the room past the bookshelves sheltering Dennis's CNS chair (she had recently heard that they may do permanent damage to the central nervous system), past the files he kept on all his clients and angels, past the police forms, until she stood behind his desk, staring at the phone's screen.

The phone r—

"Hello," she said. She recognized the man's face.

"Hello. Is Mr. Lange there, please?"

Slime. Pure slime. "No, he's not."

The man waited a moment as if expecting Kira to say something else, then said, "Oh."

"What did you want to speak to him about?" she asked.

"It's rather personal. Would you tell him that Howard Warren called? Please?"

"Why, certainly, Mr. Warren." She smiled a Dennis smile. "I'd be more than glad to relay your message if you'd be kind enough to answer one simple question for me."

"Sure. What is it?"

"You never did tell me what your preference was. Guns? Barbed wire? Bare fists?" His face grew bright red and a vein in his forehead bulged. "I like to think of you as the bare fist type," she said, stroking her chin as though she had a beard. "Yes, yes of course! How could I have been so stupid? Of course it has to be bare fists for *you*, Mr. Warren. A man like you—"

The screen went black.

Kira picked up a paperweight and threw it through the screen.

10

Freddie made Mara wait until he was sure all the other private viewing booths had emptied before he let her open the door. He made her wait until the two white-coated technicians had entered the small, blood covered room to take out his client's body. He made her wait until the walls had been washed down to their original antiseptic white. He made her wait until he was sure he wasn't going to vomit, until he was sure he had sufficient control of his emotions, until the adrenaline coursing through his system had eased off, until his pounding heart had quieted.

"Now?" she asked.

He nodded weakly. "Yeah. Now."

She stood quickly, nervously, as if what they had just witnessed had charged her up, and pressed the button next to the door. She motioned to the doorway with one hand, bowing a little, coaxing Freddie to go through first. Freddie stood, unamused, and flicked the whip-end of the riding crop across her waist.

"Shut up!" he said before she could complain or yell or react to the unwarranted blow. Freddie had just seen a man at his work, and this man's work was pleasure, and this man was the best that Freddie had ever seen. Watching Oleo Johnson like that gave Freddie something to think about.

"What time is it?" he asked.

"Two-thirty," Mara said, anger and hurt filtering through.

"If we finish up here soon enough we'll still have time to put in an appearance at Bentwell's."

She said nothing.

He led the way through the underground passageways he knew as well as every line and crease on his aging face, and stopped before a door. The hall was empty, deserted, full of dead dreams and memories that settled around Freddie's shoulders like a shroud.

He opened the door and walked through, casually glancing over his shoulder to see if Mara had followed him in. She hadn't. He smiled and nodded to a young woman sitting behind a desk near the center of the room. "Hey, Liz. You're looking good."

She smiled back. "Thanks, Freddie. It's good to see you."

"I like the way you lie," Freddie said.

She shook her head, still smiling, letting out a little sigh. "Come on, Freddie." She was an attractive woman, obviously reconstructed, yet not self-conscious about it like some people were. Her brown hair was streaked with silver and made a unique blend of old and young.

"No, I mean it. Not many people are that glad to see me lately."

"Owe a lot of money?" she asked.

"Enough."

"That could explain part of it, you know?"

He nodded, then sat in the chair by the side of her desk. She handed him a short piece of paper and he turned it over, glanced at the spaces that needed to be filled in, then took one of her pens. He jotted down the room number, client and angel's names, the necessary numbers and information on his license, noted the fee on the bottom, and put his initials beside it. He gave her back the form.

"Forgetting something?" she asked.

He leaned over and glanced at the form again. "No. It's all filled in."

She shook her head. "No, Freddie. You know what I'm talking about. The confession. We still need them, you know."

"Oh, yeah, sorry." He felt around in his pockets and smiled meekly. "I guess I left it at home, but I'd be glad to bring it by tomorrow. I've got to come by to see about a double setup I'm working on, so I could give it to you then."

"You know better than that. I don't have to read the regulations to you, do I?"

"No."

"Do you want to apply for an extension? It won't do you much good if her relatives want to fight, but it will show good faith, and that you're still trying."

"Yeah, sure, give me the form." Four-hour extensions were a joke—barely enough time to get the signed confession back to the Center and Liz. If Johnson still hadn't signed it, any legal action that might be taken as a result of the dust addict's death would leave Freddie as the named defendant. He filled out the form and slid it across the desktop.

"What's the matter, Freddie?" Liz asked.

"What?"

"Something's wrong. There's something bothering you, and I can tell that it's not just money. You've never forgotten a confession before—something must be up."

Freddie smiled and shook his head. "No. I guess it's just Mara. She and I haven't been getting along too well, lately, and my mind's been disorganized."

Liz shrugged. "You shouldn't let her get to you."

He placed a hand over hers and gave her what he thought was a sincere smile. "Thanks. It'll be okay."

She nodded.

"I've got to go—business."

"Okay, Freddie, but do me a favor, will you? Take care of yourself."

"With pleasure," Freddie said.

He walked toward the door stiffly, wondering if everyone could see the tension, the anxiety, the nervousness on his face as easily as Liz had. This thing with Lange was at the root of the whole problem—if it hadn't been for him, Freddie wouldn't have had any trouble with Johnson's confession. And now, the police might be dragged in for an investigation.

Mara was waiting for him outside the door. "Everything go all right?"

He looked at her oddly. "Why?"

"Well, you were in there for a while, and I thought something might have happened."

He shook his head. "No, nothing happened. I just have to get Oleo Johnson's confession here within four hours."

She smiled. "Forget it," she said, dismissing his concern with a wave of her hand. "We don't need his confession. No one's going to file a petition on that girl—no one out there could care about her."

"Sure," Freddie said. "You're right." But he wasn't convinced. The confession was really just a red-tape formality, good only for placing blame if and when some problem arose.

They walked out to the car.

Bentwell's place was relatively quiet, even though it was getting late. It was obvious—Freddie could tell as soon as they'd pulled into the underground garage. They took the tube up to the main entrance and looked around for a few moments, trying to place half-remembered names with familiar faces. He and Mara linked arms and walked through the main lounge.

"What did you think of him?" Freddie asked.

She knew who he was talking about immediately. "He wasn't bad at all. Do you know if he uses that glove every time?"

He shook his head. "Not that I know of. According to the person at the Center who booked the room for us, last time he used razor blades. He actually skinned—Hi there. How are you?" Freddie asked a young couple who had used his services once.

They were sitting at a small, round floating table, sipping from glasses held by hands that wore rings— rings worth twice as much as Freddie's yearly income. "Fine," the man said. He made no effort to smile or be civil and went back to the conversation he'd been having with the woman.

Freddie and Mara continued to walk around the quiet half-full lounge, nodding at a few of the regulars, checking out the newcomers.

"So?" Mara asked.

"Huh?"

"He actually skinned. . . ."

"Oh, yeah. He actually skinned an old geezer his last time out. Used razor blades. Likes to use a different weapon each time."

"He didn't make any trouble, though, did he?" she asked. "All that worrying you did was for nothing."

"It's not over yet. Her relatives still have a few hours."

"It's over, Freddie. No one's going to ask for an investigation. Besides, she was a dust addict and she signed a release."

Freddie said nothing. He applied a little pressure to her arm and steered her toward the bar.

"She did sign a release, didn't she?" Mara asked.

Freddie said nothing. Mara stopped walking and

glared at him. He stopped and turned, but refused to look her in the eyes.

"Freddie?"

"I need a drink, Mara. It's been a rough night." He turned away and continued toward the bar. She quickly caught up with him and grabbed him by the elbow.

"She did sign a release. Tell me she did, Fred."

"I'll have a screwdriver," Freddie said to the bartender. "And put a little mescanol in there, too."

"Fred?" Mara said, still by his side.

"I'm sorry, Mr. Frank, but I can't give you a drink," the bartender told him.

"What?" The bartender started to move away to ask someone else what they wanted. "Hey! What the hell are you talking about?"

Mara tugged at the back of his polo shirt. "Why? Why didn't you get her to sign a release?" Mara demanded.

"Hey!" The bartender moved back. "What the hell's going on?" Freddie demanded.

"I'm terribly sorry, Mr. Frank, but your credit has been cut off," the bartender said.

"Freddie?" Mara asked.

"Drop it!" he shouted at her. It was suddenly still around them and the silence was thick, deep, impenetrable. A nondescript man in a nondescript suit smiling a plastic smile approached.

"What seems to be the trouble?" he asked, flashing an ID and a tooth-filled smile at Freddie. The card identified him as one of Bentwell's floor managers.

Shit, Freddie thought. Just what I needed to top off a perfect evening. "The bartender seems to be mistaken. He thinks my credit's not good."

The floor manager smiled. "Oh, Mr. Frank, I'm sure it's good. You just don't have any right now."

"What's this all about?" Mara demanded.

"I'm afraid I couldn't tell you. I don't know. No

reason was given. We were told that your credit had been cut off, and if there were any problems, or if you felt there'd been a mistake—"

"You bet there's been a mistake," Freddie interrupted. "Take me to Bentwell. Right now."

The man kept his cool smile in place while he pressed the stud on his watch. Two more men as nondescript as the floor manager appeared at the fringe of the quickly gathering crowd.

"Shall we go?"

Freddie nodded, took Mara's arm, and followed Bentwell's hired goon. The other two men brought up the rear, as though Freddie and Mara were prisoners, considering a break for freedom.

"What did you do?" Mara whispered in Freddie's ear.

He sighed and looked at her imploringly. "Stuff it, will you? Please?"

They stood before the elevator tube in uncomfortable silence, waiting for the capsule to arrive at their level. Bentwell's three men kept a casual eye on Freddie and Mara, their arms dangling awkwardly by their sides, trying hard not to look too tough, too coarse, or too slick. The tube's door slid upward and they entered the clear capsule.

They rode up to Bentwell's office in silence punctuated only by one of the men's dry coughing.

Bentwell was waiting for them, sitting behind his expansive desk playing with a letter opener, an antique, turning it over and over in his hands, letting the desk light glint off its silvery surface. He waved the three men out of the office and Freddie and Mara approached the desk.

"How are you, Mara?"

"Fine," Mara said, nodding.

"And you, Freddie?"

"Not fine. Upset. And a little more than angry at your bartender. He said that my credit was no good. You ought to have a little talk with him."

Bentwell spread his arms as though there was nothing he could do to help. "It's not his fault. You shouldn't blame him for doing the job I pay him to do. If I remember correctly, a little under twenty-four hours ago, you made a deal with one of my guests downstairs in the lounge. Mr. Johnson, I believe. There is my fee to settle. . . ."

Freddie nodded. "Don't tell me you're afraid I'm going to stiff you."

Bentwell pursed his lips and shook his head slowly as if he were weary. "No, not really. One of your friends offered to cover for you if you couldn't make the fee. But you won't have any difficulty paying my fee now, will you, Mr. Frank?" he asked in a tone that left no room for doubt.

"No." Freddie's shoulders sagged a little. "Give it to me."

Bentwell smiled and leaned forward, pushing a pen across the desk to Freddie. Beneath the pen was a credit form. Freddie bent over and filled it out and pushed it back to Bentwell.

"I was planning on paying you tonight, Peter. There was no need for this fiasco."

Bentwell shrugged. "It's a tough business, Freddie."

"Our credit?" Mara asked.

Bentwell spread his arms again, this time offering them the whole place. "No problem."

"Do me a favor, will you, Peter?"

Bentwell nodded.

"Tell me who was covering for me."

"Sure. Dennis Lange."

Freddie's fists clenched. His eyes narrowed into slits, cold, angry slits, and he had trouble keeping his breathing even. "Thanks, Peter."

"Don't thank me—thank him."

"I'll do that. You know where he is now?"

"Last time I saw him, he was in the dance room."

"The dance room." He stormed out of the office,

nearly knocking Mara down. She followed him out and to the tube. "What was that all about?" she asked.

"Nothing," Freddie said in a tone that told her all she needed to know. He waited impatiently for the capsule, slapping his thigh with the riding crop, unconsciously keeping time to his heartbeat. The capsule arrived and he stepped inside, immediatcly pressing the button for the main floor. Mara managed to slip in before the door slid shut.

"Now take it easy, Freddie. Try to control yourself. Don't do anything you might—"

"Leave it, Mara!"

The capsule settled and the door opened. He walked through the lounge and entered the tube which led to the dance room. He sat in the first chair he came to and rode to the end, not thinking, not planning. Just hating.

Dennis was there, sipping a drink, sitting crosslegged on the floor. Freddie stormed over to his side and tapped him on the thigh with the toe of his boot to get Dennis's attention. It was an unnecessary action—Dennis had followed Freddie's movements from the time he entered the spherical room.

"Have a seat, Freddie."

"Like hell. I wouldn't sit down with you now, or ever. Listen, Lange—I want you to stay clear of me. Stay the hell out of my affairs. If you don't you'll be sorry. I don't need your help and I don't trust your good intentions."

"What?"

"Don't think I don't know what you're trying to do. Your little ploy was transparent. You better realize that you can't buy me in any way, shape, or form."

And without waiting for a response, Freddie turned and strode out of the dance room. Mara was waiting for him in the lounge, standing against a wall, arms crossed beneath her bare breasts, concern written all over her classically beautiful face. "Well?"

"Well, what?" he snapped.

"What did you say?"

He walked away from her, just as he'd walked away from Dennis, and went directly to the bar. The same bartender approached.

"Yes, sir?"

"Give me a screwdriver," Freddie said.

The bartender smiled, prepared the drink, and set it down before him. "Sorry about the mixup, Mr. Frank."

Freddie smiled, picked up the drink, and threw it down on the bar. "I'll have another."

11

Dennis was glad the car was on automatic and could find its way through the snaking city streets without his help. He'd had too much to drink at Bentwell's, and he had too much on his mind to have to drive. He leaned forward, opened the small, square container on the coffee table, removed a capsule, and then snapped it open under his nose. He inhaled deeply to get as much of the sobering vapor into his system as possible. A few moments later, his head was clear; even though he was physically exhausted, he was mentally alert. Or as alert as he could be after that ridiculous evening.

It had started out nicely, and Dennis had been enjoying himself, but it had quickly degenerated.

What was Freddie trying to prove? What was that scene in the dance room supposed to have been? He couldn't afford to ignore the uncomfortable feeling the evening had created. Something was going on, something he knew nothing about, something over which he had no control. Freddie's behavior made as little sense as his statements, threats, and accusations.

They'd never had a confrontation, so there was nothing for Dennis to compare it to.

Nothing.

And that was the part that disturbed him the most.

He had known Freddie for years. He'd even helped the ungrateful bastard get his start in business. There was nothing in their overlapping and entwining pasts which should have set him off like that. Nothing. Dennis was apprehensive once the initial shock and surprise had worn off. There had to be someone else involved—someone like Mara, or maybe Bentwell.

If it had been Mara, then Dennis had no idea as to what she could have said to set off Freddie like that. If it had been Bentwell, then it could have stemmed from just one thing: Dennis's offer to cover Bentwell's fee for Freddie. But that shouldn't have caused this kind of reaction. Dennis had only intended to extend a professional courtesy.

It didn't make sense.

He dimmed the lights in the car to a soft golden glow and moved over to the short couch. He stretched out as much as it would allow and tried to give his tense muscles a chance to unwind.

Freddie Frank. He wasn't the same person Dennis had known. Too many things had happened; too many people had the power to influence what he did, what he thought, how he acted. But, with all the uncertainties Dennis had about what had caused the confrontation, he was certain that he understood Freddie's warning to keep his distance. It was as though Freddie held him responsible for something that had gone wrong.

Dennis didn't need enemies. Not in his business. If staying clear would help keep things under control, help keep everyone happy, then Dennis would do it. Even if it meant not going back to Bentwell's.

When Dennis had first started as a procurer, the action was fast, the people reckless, and living was brutal, exotic, and exciting. Dennis had stood by the fringe of the super-slick set and had watched them go through their paces with a smile. It had been enticing, alluring, and magical. He'd been seduced by the rapid flow of credit, by the lightning changes in fashion, by the casual acceptance of any new vogue or attitude.

But the super-slick set in itself was no more than a group of people wearing the same facade, and the facade melted away to expose the real people underneath rather quickly. Kira had pointed it out to him, had made him face what he'd seen from the first. He'd known where the masks and roles ended and the real people began, but he'd been unwilling to face it. To confront the truth, to face what lay beneath his angels' self-deceptions meant he would have to face the truth about himself and what he did. And he'd been in no rush to do that.

Maybe that was Freddie's problem. Maybe Freddie hadn't ever faced what he did, what his angels were, and what proportion of the population they actually made up.

That was certainly Kira's problem. She never looked at the work Dennis did objectively. To her, his job began and ended with supplying rich, empty people with poor, desperate victims. She only looked at the negative side of his job—never saw the good side, the kindness and help it let him give. And they fought about it often.

She had created a lot of self-doubts in him at first, transferring her own feelings of revulsion to him. But he fought, knowing that being a procurer was more than what she made it. Without this knowledge, he realized he could have ended up like Freddie Frank.

Freddie Frank. Again. Dennis sighed, sat up, and looked through the car to the controls, checking his location on the street grid. Halfway home. He couldn't arrive soon enough. He leaned back and put his feet up on the coffee table.

Then there was Mary White. What was he supposed to do about her? He didn't particularly like the arrangement, and he knew that if Kira found out about it, living with her would be impossible. Mary White's request to become a client would reinforce Kira's dislike for his job, and he didn't need that. She would chip away at him slowly, methodically, continually, until the situation and tension built to the point where it would explode into a full-scale fight.

All those hours of countless arguments, the yelling, and his careful, precise logic, would be gone, wasted, forgotten like they had never existed. They would have to start from the beginning again. He would have to try and show her the good his job let him accomplish—the dust addicts who wanted and needed another chance; the working people who had sunk all their earnings into paying for the memory crystals; the victims of disease whose bodies were no more than mockeries of the human form; none of them would have had any hope of reconstruction if it weren't for procurers.

How was a person eighty years old living on government subsistence, who had an updated crystal—a faithful duplicate of their memories and personality —but who had no money left over for reconstruction going to get a second life? Without someone's help, without someone paying the charge for transferring the crystal's information into a new body, the person would die.

And for each client, each victim Dennis led into those clean white rooms, each human being he gave to the sexually maladjusted angels, a new birth occurred. A reconstructed person. It was the only way to look at it.

71

He tried to make it as simple and easy on everyone involved as possible. Some clients needed preparation to make them more acceptable for Dennis's angels—some rest, food, some counseling, or maybe just a few reassuring words. Whatever it was, Dennis made sure each and every one of his clients understood and got what they needed to make it through the experience. He was good at removing some of their fear and trauma.

The point he liked to stress the most, the point that helped his clients develop the proper attitude, was that of awakening after reconstruction. He would tell them that they would wake up with mind and personality intact in a fresh, young body without any memory of the experience of being a victim. Even if their crystals were updated a few seconds before they walked into the small white rooms, none of what happened after the last update would be remembered. And that was what ultimately let the system work.

None of the pain, discomfort, humiliation, horror, shame or terror of being a client was remembered. None of it had been recorded in the crystal.

Some of Dennis's clients had even looked him up after reconstruction to thank him for helping them get a second life. One of them had been curious enough to ask what Dennis's angel had done to them, but Dennis wrote that off as a maso reaction, or a perverse sense of curiosity.

But Mary White just wouldn't fall into that nice, neat stereotypical client mold. Granted, like all the others, she did it for the money, but that was where the similarities ended. She didn't need the money for reconstruction—she needed it for something else. Whether for a gambling debt, a new car, a vacation, to replace her cut-off allowance, or for the maso experience, her reasons clearly set her apart from the norm. And Dennis wasn't sure he liked that.

He knew all too well what Kira would say if she found out. He was glad he'd left her at home, out of the thick of things, where her bias wouldn't interfere with his business.

The car slowed and made several sharp, familiar turns. He would be home in a few minutes. He rubbed his face with his hands, trying to erase some of the fatigue, the bone-tired weariness that was piled on layer after layer, night after night. It wasn't something he could shake off with a good night's sleep—it went deeper, too deep, and stemmed from anxieties which had developed over years of dealing with the same kind of people.

Mary White was going to cause more trouble than she was worth. It would probably be best not even to mention her to Kira, and run the risk of Kira finding out on her own. To tell her now would only give her further ammunition for a fresh fight about a stale argument.

The car stopped; the roof slid back and the doors formed exit ramps. Dennis walked into his house.

There was something wrong, and he stopped before the living room, glancing around, trying to detect what was disturbing him. The room was a little darker than usual. Glass on the floor. Large shards floating in the suspensor field by the couch. No lamp. Kira.

"Kira?" he shouted.

No response. He waited a moment, shouted for her again, and still got no answer. He walked into the living room and found pieces of a smashed drinking glass on the floor beneath a painting. He shook his head slowly, fighting back the anger rising in him like flames making their way up a tree trunk. He gritted his teeth and made a search of the rooms.

He found her in his den, sitting in the CNS chair. There would be no point in rushing her—she would come out of the experience disoriented if he shut if off now, and it would probably take her more time to readjust to his presence than if he just let the program finish. He sat down behind his desk to wait.

Then he saw the smashed phone screen. What the hell had happened? What was it with her? If it wasn't one thing it was something else. He sighed, the air escaping his lips in short, tight exhalations. The message light was on, triggered by the incoming call. He wouldn't be able to see the caller's face when he replayed it, but the conversation should have been recorded. He pressed the playback button.

Kira's voice first, then a man's, almost recognized, definitely familiar. Kira's tone was offensive and sarcastic. The man mentioned his name and Dennis smashed the desk with his fist. Howard Warren. She had done it again, without even leaving the house.

He stormed out of the room and went into their bedroom. He sat on the chair near the bed and swiveled the phone screen. He tried Howard Warren's number. The phone rang several times before he realized the time—he immediately regretted calling at this hour. It could have waited. A plain, washed-out, middle-aged woman's image appeared on the screen. She was dressed in a sheer, unattractively revealing nightgown.

"May I speak with Mr. Warren, please?"

"Your name?" she asked, stifling a yawn.

"Dennis Lange."

A pause while she thought something over, then a hesitant, "He's not home. Leave your number and I'll tell him to call you when he gets in."

"No, that's all right. I'll call back. When do you think I could reach him? It's rather important."

She laughed softly. "Important? I'll tell him you called."

He saw her hand reaching for the cut-off switch near the screen right before it went black.

Kira. Thanks. There goes the perfect angel for Mary White. Warren's a total novice and he probably

74

wouldn't have hurt her that much. Now I've got a goddamned mess on my hands.

He got up slowly, deliberately, and walked back into his den to yank Kira out of the CNS chair, to let her know just how happy she had made him.

12

Oleo's long, bony fingers tapped out the rhythm of a mnemonic ditty like capering marionettes set free from their strings. The ditty ran through his head, down his fingers and back like an infectious disease corrupting his thoughts, crumbling his powers of concentration. Oleo wished the person who had devised the pathological tune would walk into his office. He would not walk out. Carried out, perhaps, he thought. But he'd be too dead to walk.

Oleo was outwardly calm, yet he looked around the room furtively. There was more than the mnemonic eating away at his mind; most of the anxiety centered around that short European who'd sauntered into his office demanding his feet be kissed. Berkoff. Only Oleo had found out, when he'd arrived at the office that morning, that Berkoff's real name was Berkman. George Berkman.

The slum apartment in the downtown area he had entered was rented under the name Berkman. Oleo's operative had followed the man to work and found out he was a clerk at the Administration Complex earning just enough money to keep up the payments on his crystal and get by. The report the operative had handed in was spread out on Oleo's desk.

Oleo glanced at the meticulously prepared pages, following George Berkman's actions for the last twenty-four hours. That, along with the summary research at the end of the report, provided enough information to make Oleo feel unsettled and anxious.

The person Berkman had portrayed didn't exist, and was a hastily prepared cover. Working in the Administration Complex gave Berkman the opportunities he would have needed to prepare a false identification, but he wasn't far enough up the ladder to make the cover go deep enough to withstand any serious inquiries. There was no money behind him, no overseas investment conglomerates, no chance of Oleo getting into the financial aspects of the Centers.

Then what was behind Berkman's ridiculous appointment? Why would he have tried to fool Oleo when, the moment his cover or credentials were checked, he would be shown for who he really was?

He could be an investigator, Oleo thought. He could be checking me out—trying to find out if I'm involved in any illegal or unprofessional practices. Well, even if he did turn out to be an investigator, there would be nothing to worry about. There was nothing wrong with Oleo's business.

That settled it. He would have to get in touch with Berkman to find out who he was and what was going on. He could have let the matter rest, and he thought that would have been the wisest course but for one thing: the name Berkman was vaguely familiar. The name carried an association—distant, remote, and buried beneath years of memories.

Berkman.

Oleo shook his head. Not nice, he thought. Not nice at all.

Either Oleo would have to play, or wait for Berkman to make the next move. Waiting was what Berkman wanted—that much was obvious. He would have developed a better cover and background if he'd expected Oleo to check him out.

Then it was decided. Oleo would grab the initiative he'd developed by having Berkman followed; he would make the next move.

He entered the number for the Complex into the phone and waited for the circuit to complete. The in-house operator appeared on Oleo's phone screen. He asked for George Berkman and waited while she rang his extension. Berkman appeared, slightly puzzled and very apprehensive.

Oleo smiled for the phone screen's lens. "Well, Mr. Berkoff. How nice. I tried to get hold of you at your hotel, but. . . ."

"What do you want, Johnson?" Berkman demanded. His face was livid, his hands trembling, his eyes darting to sights and sounds out of the screen's range.

"Have you found another broker yet?" Oleo asked, keeping his face a mask of placidity.

Berkman's expression seemed to reflect his thoughts. Oleo could see him speeding down lines of thought, considering insane possibilities, like Oleo's not really knowing that Berkoff was a cover, or Oleo's somehow getting in touch with him at work to discuss investments, but ruled that out instantly. "No. No, I haven't," he said, falling back into Berkoff's speech pattern and mannerisms.

Oleo laughed long, hard, and brutally at the man. Berkman did not smile and Oleo quieted slowly, catching his breath, wiping the tears collecting at the corners of his eyes. "Why don't you drop it, Berkman?" Oleo asked. "What's this all about?"

"I didn't *think* you'd remember," he spat.

"Remember? What am I supposed to remember, Berkman? Some lousy investment I made for you?

Some scheme you and some friends were working on to take me for a bundle? What, Berkman? What?"

Berkman glared back, fists clenched, breathing deeply, ready to explode. "Ruth."

Oleo was stunned for a moment, trying to absorb what Berkman had said and its significance.

"Ruth," he repeated. When he saw no recognition of the name appear on Oleo's face, he told him. "She was my daughter, Johnson. Ruth Berkman. But I don't suppose you'd remember that. It happened a long time ago."

Ruth Berkman? Ruth Berkman? What in all hell was he talking about? Oleo wondered. This is getting out of hand. "I don't know what you're talking about."

"You should. You killed her."

"I did?"

"Yes. And you killed her in one of the most obscene, vile, filthy, cruel and inhuman ways possible."

"Now wait a minute, Berkman," Oleo said, suppressing his mounting pride and excitement. "Maybe I did kill her. But if I did, I paid for the right to do it, and that means doing it any way I want. She wanted to be a victim."

"You killed her and you're going to pay," Berkman said calmly, as though ordering breakfast.

"You're sick, you know that? You need help."

"You killed her, Johnson."

This was crazy. Oleo slapped out and hit the button that severed the connection. The blank screen stared at him. He felt as though it were trying to tell him something, show him something, but his mind was already working on Berkman, too busy to listen to the reflection of his unconscious.

Berkman was insane. Without question, totally, raving, insane. How could he hold Oleo responsible for his daughter's death? She'd been a client. Oleo hadn't approached her on the street. Oleo hadn't lured her into a Center. Oleo hadn't been the procurer. Oleo hadn't asked for Ruth Berkman above all other clients available at that time. It had just happened that way, and from what little Oleo could remember and figure out, it had happened almost five full years ago.

Berkman must have been watching the whole thing from one of the private viewing booths—Ruth must have been the one that freaked out the minute Oleo had walked into the small white room. She had torn all the clothes from his body and had finally gotten to his hood. She'd ripped it off and raked her nails across his face and had gotten him angry. Ruth and the fifteen-year-old dust addict had been the only victims who had seen his face.

If Berkman did hold him responsible, why had he waited five years before doing something about it? And if Berkman really planned to mete out some sort of revenge, why had he warned Oleo by showing up as Berkoff?

He shook his head.

Not nice. Not nice at all.

Well, there were ways to deal with people like that. There was the police. Maybe a call to them would help. They might warn Berkman that they were aware of the threat he'd made. And that might prove to be enough.

But even as he reached to punch the button on the phone that would put him into contact with the police, he realized that a warning from them wouldn't be enough. Five years was a long time—time enough for hatred and revenge to twist a mind, to warp memories and emotions. Time enough for an insane plan of revenge.

"Police," the speaker beneath his screen announced.

"I'd like to report a threat on my life," Oleo said. He felt foolish, self-conscious.

"Hold on, please."

A click, then the ringing of an extension. Oleo

broke the connection. The police would be next to worthless.

But there was something he could do.

He dialed the number.

"Hello?" the half-asleep voice said.

"Hello, Freddie. How you doin'?"

"Fine," Freddie said, suddenly alert through an almost-swallowed yawn. "How'd you like that dust addict? Nice, huh?"

Oleo nodded. "Very nice. So nice, in fact, I'd like to use your services again."

Freddie beamed a smile. "Sure."

"But there's just one problem. . . ."

"Yeah?"

"There's something bothering me."

"Yeah?"

Oleo nodded again. "And when there's something bothering me, I can't really let myself go. I can't get in the right mood. I'd be thinking about my problem all the time. Is there anything you could do to help?"

Freddie nodded confidently. "I don't see why not." He rubbed his eyes and swallowed a yawn. "Let me wake up a bit and I'll come over to your office. I presume your problem concerns a person?"

"Yes."

"Well, I'll come over there and get all the information I'll need."

"Good," Oleo said. He gave him the address, then broke the connection.

He leaned back in his chair, pushed himself away from the desk, and stretched out his legs. He'd been right in leaving the police out of this and calling Freddie Frank. He was a person who'd do just about anything—if the money was right.

His secretary buzzed him, then walked into his office.

"Yes, Susan?"

"Your first appointment is here, Mr. Johnson."

"Very good. Show him in."

When Freddie Frank arrived, Oleo saw how badly he fit in—he clashed with the furnishings, the office workers, and the building itself. He was a shepherd, and flowing in his wake were swarms of imperceptible, subliminal roaches and rats. Frank was slime in his own environment; his presence in Oleo's office just made the sliminess that much stronger, thanks to the glaring contrast.

Oleo pointed to one of the chairs, the one upholstered in easy-washable-guaranteed-not-to-pick-up-the-smell vinyl, and Freddie slithered over and oozed his way into it. Oleo shook his head, trying to clear it of the ridiculous images.

"Good of you to come so soon," Oleo said, sitting behind his desk.

Freddie leered, drooled saliva from the corner of his mouth. Oleo blinked; the leer and drool disappeared, replaced by a normal smile. Too much mescanol with lunch? Must be, he realized.

"I just hope I'll be able to help out."

"I hope so, too."

"Nice office," Freddie said, glancing around, checking it out, mentally comparing it to other offices he'd been in.

"His name is Berkman. George Berkman," Oleo said, wanting to get the encounter over with as quickly as possible. "He works at the Administration Complex."

Freddie's eyebrows rose and he pursed his lips in a silent whistle. "Status?"

"Clerk."

"Oh." His baby face wrinkled in confusion. "What's the problem, then? A clerk shouldn't be connected with you, Mr. Johnson."

"Shouldn't. That's the right word: shouldn't. Only, this clerk is, and I don't like it. Seems as if I had his daughter as a victim a number of years ago, and he's decided he resents that."

"I know just how to handle him. One of my wife's

ex-husbands holds a respectable and powerful position in the Complex. It may cost some money, but I'm sure Henri could be persuaded to ... let's say, *lean* on him a little?"

Oleo shook his head. "Not strong enough. This Berkman's gone over the deep end. He's been carrying this grudge for five years. It's got to be something a little stronger. Something a little more ... permanent?"

Oleo hoped he hadn't said too much. What he was implying was highly illegal and its penalties were harsh: death. He just hoped he'd said enough for the dense blob of human flesh seated across from him to get the drift. He didn't want to have to spell it out.

"I see," Freddie said. "Just how permanent did you have in mind?"

Oleo passed a blank credit-check across the desk. Freddie picked it up, saw the date, signature, credit number, and his name written in as payee. He definitely got the drift.

"That permanent, huh?"

Oleo nodded.

Freddie folded the check and tossed it across the desk. It fluttered down in front of Oleo, half open. Oleo took it hard—Frank had been his best shot. Without him, Oleo would have to rely on the police, a lot of good luck, or just do it himself. When he looked up, though, Frank was smiling. Obscenely.

"I think we can work something out. Something that should be ... mutually beneficial?"

Oleo's eyebrows rose. "Oh?"

Freddie smiled and nodded.

13

It wasn't that he was married to her—there were always alternatives to marriage. Divorce, living together, murder with reconstruction, open relationships, group marriages, communal marriages; the laws made it easier for people who chose not to marry, and even easier for those who did not have children. From what Dennis could discern through his observations, marriage was something like fashion: some years anything was acceptable, some years something new was in vogue.

But he knew they couldn't have stayed married if they hadn't really loved each other. Somewhere, buried beneath the layers of scar tissue the years of fighting had left inside Kira, he knew she loved him.

And the problem was that he really loved her, too. It would have been so much easier if he hadn't.

But he wasn't stuck with her, and he didn't feel as though he were. That was the point he tried to keep in mind whenever he wanted to throttle her, or throw her from a balcony to see her pinwheel in slow motion to the concrete hundreds of meters below. He could always leave. She could always leave. The only thing that kept them together was themselves.

They walked into the nearest mall entrance. Kira didn't want to shop—there was nothing she needed, and Dennis could have thought of better places to spend his afternoon. But the mall held memories for them; it was a physical link with a happier past, a neutral ground. He'd taken her to this mall on their first date and they'd sat and talked, walked and talked, shopped and talked all evening.

The double doors slid open as they approached and they were hit with a blast of dry, stale, chilled air, laced with the scents of thousands of bodies, spiced with artificial perfumes, colognes, after shaves, and deodorants, suffused with noise—raucous, overpowering noise—making their first breath of the mall's air vibrant and electrifying.

When Kira had suggested they spend their afternoon in the mall, Dennis had readily agreed. He'd figured that anything would be better than sitting around the house with her, waiting for an opportunity to tell her what he had wanted to tell her last night. One wrong word from her and the pulsating pool of anger would be unlocked and start to flow. He would have said something to her, something would have happened, something that he would have probably regretted. The mall was infinitely superior.

He slipped his arm through hers and they walked inside. The mall was a medium-sized shopping plaza —there were two others in the city that were nearly twice this size. It was six kilometers long, three kilometers wide. It was crowded, as usual, but Dennis expected that. They waited for a minute, until there was a break in the flow of constantly moving bodies, then forged ahead into the swarming mass.

Bodies sweated, groaned, mumbled, chattered, spat curses and hurled invectives, jammed elbows into other bodies' ribs and stomachs, stepped on toes and heels, milled around, looked for unsuspecting marks, dragged younger, undeveloped bodies by the hand to keep them out of trouble. Kira was knocked in the face with a hand and she managed to kick the body connected to it without being caught.

Each store had its own music, its own ditty, a carefully composed tune that would separate it from all the others. The mnemonics were played through speakers above the doorways. Some stores, the ones with more offensive theme songs, were missing speakers. Dennis liked visiting these stores—somewhere inside them was a clue to why their ditties were so offensive, why people had ripped down their speakers.

The mass of bodies was less dense toward the center of the mall, and Kira was slowly but surely angling them toward it. Dennis yanked hard on her arm—a little too hard, he realized, and she stopped and turned to face him. The churning, throbbing mass of bodies separated, parted and flowed around them slowly, ponderously.

"Where are we going?" Dennis asked.

"Just to the edge. I want to see the river."

"Again?"

"What do you mean, again? We didn't even look the last time we came here."

The river was where he'd proposed to her. He nodded, swallowing the answer he'd orginally wanted to use. "Let's ride, though, okay?"

She shook her head. "Walk there, ride back."

He sighed. "Lead on."

The closer they got to the river, the easier the going became. It took them nearly an hour to walk the kilometer and, although Dennis was pleased to get there, he was ready to turn around and head back almost immediately.

There were few stores near the mall's center, and no apartments at all. The majority of the shops lined the walls and formed avenues. Kira spotted an empty spot by the railing and dragged Dennis along. She pointed downward.

There were trees beneath the thick layer of glass. Leaves fluttered in an artificial wind, stirring their branches to sway in intricate, hypnotic patterns. The wind parted and bent the grass, the tall weeds, and the flowers by the roots of the trees. The river flowed through the center, visible through the spaces between the trees' branches, through the clearings, and carried tiny boats filled with little people, sightseeing, vacationing in the mall, relaxing, or just amusing themselves. Long, wild reeds grew by the river bank, forever bent under the flowing water's pressure, yet never yielding, never through fighting for their right to stand tall and grow straight.

Although Dennis couldn't see them, he knew animals were down there, living, feeding, procreating, dying beneath the meter-thick glass.

It was soothing to watch the movement—trees, water, and grass, synchronized in some vast plan, flying insects, burrowing animals, fish. Dennis shook his head. It was hard to believe. A totally enclosed environment, complete with a flowing river within its one by two kilometer boundaries.

The way the river always moved, the way the reeds were bent back, the way the trees swayed, the—

"Let's go down there. Let's take a boat ride," Kira said.

Her voice was soft, gentle, tender, caressing, and it rekindled a mood Dennis thought he'd lost long ago, lost through the fights, the things said but never meant . . . she sounded like she had when they'd first met. Her tone washed his anger away, letting him look at her and truly see her as she really was for the first time in years.

He was surprised. She was and was not the same person he'd always known. Slight signs of age were obvious around her eyes, her mouth, but they were complimentary, adding a maturity to her beauty he'd never seen before. She'd lost some of her pixyishness, some cuteness, and had developed into a beautiful woman.

He reached out to touch her.

Electric.

She moved closer.

Dennis's chest congested, and he felt the place inside himself he'd kept locked for years open. "To hell with the river. Let's go home. Now."

She smiled at him, and he saw something he thought was gone forever: warmth in her green, deep eyes.

As the car drove them home, they made love. Tenderly, slowly, caringly—techniques of love neither of them had had the patience, interest, or inclination to use for a long time.

Dennis was certain. After all the arguments, all the fights, all the aggravation, all the misunderstandings, the silent, bitter grudges, physical reactions to things that shouldn't have been reacted to, they still loved each other. He was certain.

There was still a chance of his getting her to understand what he was doing, what he wanted to do, of trying to resolve some of the bitterness she harbored toward him because of his job, of getting her on the right track, on a healthy track, of making the relationship live and grow again.

His anger ebbed.

He dressed, thinking about how the dreams they had shared while starting out their lives together had become mangled with time. To go back was impossible. To find a single point, a single action, a single word, thought, or situation where the change had taken place was impossible. To go over and over—

"Dennis?" she asked, placing a warm hand on his bare shoulder.

He turned.

"What were you thinking about?"

"Us," he said, almost choking on the word. "Just us. What happened, what we are now, what we used to be."

"I want it to be like it was before, Dennis. I don't want to fight any more. I don't like fighting."

He sighed. "I know what you mean, baby, but it'll never be the same. It'll never be like that."

"It could," she said slowly, cautiously, testing and tasting the words as she spoke them.

He knew what was coming.

"You could quit. We've got enough money to live the rest of our lives in comfort."

"I know, I know. The crystals are paid for, and the Center has the money we'll need for reconstruction. So we're well off, right?"

"Then why won't you stop?"

"It bothers you that much?" he asked, realizing immediately that his being a procurer did bother her that much, that it was the crux of their problem, that it was the thing ruining their relationship, their marriage, that it ate away at Kira every night, like a cancer. He knew then that if he quit, their marriage could return to something he had thought was long dead, long forgotten, remembered only in half-dreams.

"Yes," she said, still sounding like the old Kira, like the Kira Dennis had fallen in love with and had wanted to marry although marriage hadn't been in vogue at the time. "It does."

All right, then. I'll quit, he thought.

Her hand tightened on his shoulder as she waited for his reply. But just quitting like that didn't feel right to him. It was impulsive, risky, illogical, and against what he really wanted to do. For all of its negative aspects, he enjoyed his job, found it interesting and challenging. It gave him a chance to meet and help people.

"All right, Kira. I can't quit yet, but I suppose I

should be honest and tell you that I've been considering giving it up. I'm not just saying this for your benefit, either. There'd be no sense in that—if I didn't think that quitting was a viable possibility, I'd just continue fighting with you about it. I don't want to fight about it anymore."

"You mean that?"

"I do."

"I love you, Dennis."

"You're just saying that because it's true." But she didn't smile, and his joke hung in the air, making him regret saying it. "I'm sorry, baby. I love you, too."

The car pulled into their garage.

They headed straight for the bedroom.

14

Making love with Kira could be just that—love. The act itself could transcend the physical sensations, the feeling of release. It could be a true manifestation of the love they shared. It had been like that when they were first married, when they had honeymooned —and after what Dennis had just experienced in the bedroom and the car, he knew it could be like that again, and again, and again.

He felt a little less alone, a little less like it was Dennis Lange against the world.

Kira had done things to his body, things that had reached some hidden, unreleased, atavistic part of his mind, heart, and soul that had lain dormant for years. Years. And there had been no need for extreme pain, for hurting, for torture, for domination—there was still enough kinkiness in being married, being in love, being in bed together, still sharing and enjoying each other's touch, each other's flesh.

Dennis sat up slowly, so he wouldn't disturb her. She was resting peacefully—perhaps more peacefully than she had for a long time. She looked beautiful: arms outstretched; legs twisted in the sheets; makeup smudged. Even though she wasn't as pretty as she was dressed up, ready to go out, her hair shining, her makeup tastefully underdone, she was real and human like this. He eased off the bed and dressed quietly.

He felt like humming, or whistling, or rushing back to the bed to embrace her, hug her, feel her warmth next to his skin, but he suppressed these urges and desires and walked out of the room.

Perhaps a part of why their relationship had come to life again had to do with last night, he thought. The crowd at Bentwell's had been less of a strain on his nerves since he'd known she was at home.

He walked into his den. The deep colors and subdued lighting intensified and reinforced the mellow warmth inside of him. He suddenly became aware that his stomach no longer hurt, that his body wasn't wound up to the breaking point, that he wasn't gnashing his teeth together.

He selected a program card at random from the bookshelves around the CNS chair, and slipped it into the slot. It went in with a satisfying click. He eased himself down onto the soft cushions and pressed the button...

... and was weightless, floating womblike, turning cartwheels and somersaults with infinite ease and grace. White noise wrapped around his body like a cocoon, permeating the air, generated by a communications speaker behind a grill in the ship's control console. The Mars Colonies were still too far away to be anything but a series of numbers on the radar and navigational screens. It was up to Dennis to set the ship down safely, to convert the numbers on the screens into a real bubble-dome on the Martian surface.

He pushed off a near bulkhead and drifted over to the console. He grabbed hold of the top of the acceleration couch and maneuvered himself under the restraining straps. Instruments and controls pinged, beeped warnings, flashed lights in his eyes as reminders of knobs that needed turning, switches that needed throwing. Computer simulations and constructs took up the main screen before his eyes, showing him his relationship to the planet's axis and rotation.

He knew which buttons to press—he had been doing this all his adult life—and the ship entered a stable orbit. The air was rich, pure, invigorating; the sounds were varied, textured, stimulating.

A hand on his shoulder.

He turned slowly, calmly, smiling in anticipation of who he knew his co-pilot would be.

"Everything's been taken care of," Kira said. "Everything but us, that is."

Dennis slipped out from beneath the restraining straps and reached out for her. His momentum caused them to drift apart, yet they managed to entwine their fingers, held together by the slightest pressure, until they floated together and embraced.

Her naked body felt cool and soft.

Love in freefall was not the simplest thing, but they managed, arms and legs wrapped around each other like two spiders, moving in ways they'd always thought impossible, feeling areas stimulated that had never before transmitted anything but the sensation of being crushed—

His den was dark; Kira stood in the doorway.

"Hungry?" she asked. She wore a light blue wrap that was just translucent enough, exposing the curve of her firm, small breasts.

Dennis nodded. "Yes, a little. Give me about half an hour and I'll help prepare the food."

"Fine." She drifted out of the doorway and down the hall.

There were a few things Dennis wanted to take

care of before he left for work. He rose, pulled the card out of the CNS chair, replaced it in its case, then sat behind his desk. He immediately made a note to have the phone screen repaired, then looked up Howard Warren's number. He thought of using the phone before him, but decided against it; he wanted to apologize to Warren, and that was something that had to be done visually as well as verbally. It was no longer a question of keeping Warren as an angel—Dennis had given up on that. But if Warren hadn't been insulted by Kira's assault, and if an apology would be enough to smooth things over, Dennis wouldn't complain. He could use Howard Warren for Mary White. He made a note of the number and went into the kitchen.

Kira was standing by the terminal on the counter, watching the list of foods inventoried in the house's pantries. He sat in the breakfast nook and wished he'd brought along a pillow to cushion the hard, uncomfortable, wooden seat. He swung the screen around.

He pressed the number. While the phone rang, he glanced at Kira; she was watching him, leaning against the counter, arms folded over her breasts. A click, then Warren's face filled the screen.

"Hello, Mr. Warren," Dennis said.

"I'm not in."

"Pardon me?"

"I said I'm not in, Lange. Don't bother me."

The knot in Dennis's stomach started to bloom like an ugly cactus. "I just called to apologize, Mr. Warren. I wasn't going to—"

"Not interested, Lange. I've found another procurer."

"Who's that?" a woman's voice asked off-screen, dripping sarcasm and barely disguised disgust. "Another one of your new high-classed friends?"

"Shut up, Paula," Warren said to his left.

"Well, Mr. Warren, as I said—I'm not calling to solicit business. I don't work that way. I just don't like

94

the manner in which you were treated. It was unjusti-
fied, and angel or not, I feel I owe you an apology."

"Hang up, Lange. You don't owe me a thing. And
don't bother me anymore. If you want to talk, call me
at work. You *do* have business with the Complex,
don't you?"

Dennis shrugged. He sighed then smiled and
looked into the man's nervous, darting eyes. "Best of
luck to you, then. I hope you find what you're looking
for."

"Save it. Save the apology, and save your luck.
You're going to need them."

Dennis broke the connection. He felt like he'd
been hit, dragged by a car, totally wrung out by two
massive hands. Kira walked over and looked at him
imploringly. "I'm sorry," she said. "I really am."

"It's okay."

"Would you like me to call? Maybe I could set
things straight."

"You've done enough as it is." The knot in his
stomach doubled as he realized what he'd just said. It
was starting again. He slid out from the booth and
embraced her. She reacted stiffly. "Hey, I'm sorry. I
didn't mean that. I really didn't. It was ... habit." She
softened a little. "It's not going to be easy for me. The
patterns go deep, and they're hard to change. They
can be very destructive if we're not careful."

"I understand. How about eating?"

"Sure," he said, leading her back to the counter.

They watched the menu roll by on the terminal,
as the food unit decided what meals could be prepared from the available inventory.

Toward the end of the meal, the tension couldn't
be ignored. It had started off easily, smoothly, but, as
time passed, Kira became edgy. Dennis would be
going to Bentwell's and would be facing the same,
nightly decision. He wanted to postpone it until the
last possible moment in an attempt to preserve the

quiet, peaceful atmosphere. And he really wasn't sure whether or not he wanted her to go with him.

It could be good—she could control her drinking and intake of drugs if she wanted to and, by doing so, could stay out of trouble. It wasn't that much to ask, but if anything did go wrong, whatever closeness they had gained would be lost.

The meal ended in silence, and Dennis retreated to his den. As he sat behind his desk, he remembered Mary White and realized that Kira shouldn't go along to Bentwell's tonight. Once Mary's deal had been properly set up and was no longer in the talking stages, Kira could go with him. But not until. To take the risk of running into Mary while Kira was by his side . . . well, better not take the chance.

He touched his thumb to the lock on the bottom desk drawer. It clicked and slid open to give him access to his files. Selecting just the right person for Mary required finding an angel who was willing to pay, and pay, and pay.

Dennis knew he would have to cook up something special, something out of the ordinary, but that would be the least of his problems. He'd devised insane, complicated situations for some of his less imaginative angels. They had come to rely on Dennis's creativity. Props, time limits, harassment—whatever he decided on, Mary's setup had to be good. He was planning on charging the highest possible fee and then tagging on the amount Mary wanted for herself. It was the only way it could be done.

After looking over his files and eliminating those who were into specific fetishes, those who had certain price limits, and those who were of the wrong sex, only one angel fit the requirements better than the others. Albert Johnson. Dennis removed his file to look it over.

The only negative point to Johnson was his extreme taste for violence—ultra violence. There were violent angels, and then there were violent angels.

And there was Albert Johnson. There was a norm, a level of violence common to most angels. Dennis figured that Howard Warren would have been on the least-violent end of the scale; but he knew that Albert Johnson stood alone at the opposite end.

Alone. With any weapon short of a neutron bomb. Alone in a white room with a client. A victim. Mary White.

Dennis shrugged and jotted down Johnson's numbers. He checked his watch—it was late enough for Johnson to be home, and scratched off his office number. He didn't want to call from the kitchen or from the bedroom. They were the only screens in working order, but he didn't want to give Kira the opportunity to overhear or walk in on the conversation. There was no need for that. None at all. It would only start up the old problems again.

He scanned the files once more to double-check his first choice, but still found no one within the normal violence range willing to pay the fee he would have to charge.

Once he'd made up his mind, Dennis didn't care what Mary needed the money for. That was her business. It was his business to make sure that everything went well, and that she got what she wanted. Or needed. Or in this case, something entirely different. Something named Albert "Oleo" Johnson.

He had to take the car to the nearest public phone. He'd told Kira that he had an errand to run; she'd been cooperatively uncurious and trusting. If she continued to be sympathetic for a little while longer, he thought he might actually quit. Of course he'd have to find something equally as interesting with the same facets as procuring, but he was sure that if and when he wanted to, he could find some other line of work.

He put the car on manual as he searched for a public phone in working order. The first phone he'd spotted had been smashed beyond repair. He spotted one a block away on his right, and yanked hard on the steering lever. The car wouldn't go where he wanted; he glanced to his right, through the window, and saw a car traveling beside him. He smiled and patted the console's safety circuits, thankful that they'd worked properly. He'd heard about what the teenagers were doing—disconnecting the units to get their thrills from near-collisions and bent metal.

His car slowed. The one on his right pulled ahead and Dennis's car moved into the right lane. He stopped it before the public phone. It looked operational, so he pressed the "park" button. The car parked itself, the roof slid back, and he was at the phone before the ramps touched the ground.

He inserted his ID card into the slot, entered his credit number, pressed the phone number, and waited.

Oleo's long, drawn, equine face filled the screen. "Hello?"

"Hi. Remember me?" Dennis asked, joking.

Oleo froze. His expression remained, as though it had been frozen in liquid helium, complete with bulging eyes holding the distinct look of naked fear. Almost immediately, the expression melted away to distraction, then a cool composure. Dennis wasn't sure he'd really seen it. "Sure, Dennis. Very funny. What can I do for you?"

"Did I catch you at a bad time?"

"What do you mean?"

"Well, you looked a little shaken up. I thought that something might be wrong. I can call back. . . ."

"No, no. Nothing's wrong." Oleo forced a thin smile. It looked wooden. "What is it?"

"Maybe some other time, Al. I don't want to bother you, and it's important enough—well, it's too important to tell you about if you're in a bad mood."

Oleo's eyebrows arched. "Hold on a moment, will you?"

Dennis nodded. Oleo's image was immediately replaced by a kaleidoscopic display, accompanied by a current pop tune. He was gone for almost two minutes.

"Sorry about the delay, Dennis. What did you have in mind?"

"I've got a client—someone very special. I thought you might be interested . . ."

"How special?"

Dennis smiled. "Why don't we meet someplace—have a drink? You busy?"

"No," Oleo said hesitantly. "I've got some time."

"Come on down to Bentwell's tonight, then. Okay?"

"Okay. Can't you tell me anything?"

Dennis smiled. "Just that she's a regular there."

Oleo beamed a smile.

Dennis hung up. There was something wrong with Johnson. He'd acted uncomfortable, as though he were afraid of something Dennis might say or do. He'd never seen Johnson act like that before. First Freddie, now Oleo.

Now Dennis was certain.

Something *was* going on.

15

Sleek, like a black beast of the night, Oleo thought, as he watched himself in the mirror. Mean. Double-dirty. Very, very bad. Extra large size, extra large trouble.

He paraded for his eyes, for the generations of Johnsons yet unborn, primping and preening and pumping himself up, reveling in the way he looked, the way he moved. The guise of stockbroker had fallen away like ash, like scabs, like a skin shed by a reptile. He no longer had to kiss ass and bow and scrape and humble himself to get his slice of the investment monies. Not for now, anyway. Tomorrow —well, there were years before tomorrow came, before he had to go back and lick boots.

He was dressed as he always saw himself, the way he thought of his heart—in black. And with the shoulder pads, the chest expander, the girdle for his slightly-sagging middle, and the stuffing in his pants in just the right places, he looked how he felt.

He could squash Lange's deranged head with his bare hands as if it were a melon. He could twist his head right off his neck as if it were a bottle cap. He could take his body apart piece by piece like a man eating a lobster.

Who did Lange think he was, messing around with Oleo? he asked himself. Oleo. He spoke the name out loud, letting it roll off his tongue, flow out of his mouth and soar through the air like a magnificent bird of prey. Oleo. A name he was proud of, a name few people had the nerve to use around him.

Oleo.

He slipped his thumbs into his vest pockets, letting his fingers hang down like strands of steel cable. His right thumb touched the reassuring piece of metal—cold, unforgiving metal. The metal of a needle gun's handle. It was a weapon easily hidden in a small pocket, like that of a vest, or palmed when needed in a hurry.

Why bother taking Lange apart piece by piece and get himself messed up when the needle gun could do the job instantly, silently, with no effort? He didn't want to use it, but if Lange had found out what they'd planned and this meeting was just an excuse for a confrontation, then Oleo would be ready. He might have to shoot him. And that would be nice. Very nice.

He pulled the gun out of his pocket to check the sliver-thin needles.

Yellow: Stun needles.

That would be fine. Just fine. They'd dissolve within five seconds of impact, after having released their chemicals. No need to kill the poor bastard. Not yet, anyway.

16

Bentwell's: Three floors of curiosities for the bored; two holorooms; a spherical dance room; two restaurants; twenty-four bedrooms for the anxious; four office suites; an underground parking garage; a main lounge large enough to get lost in, and four smaller, more intimate lounges. Each lounge had two separate bars—one for alcholic drinks, one for drugs —at least ten private niches, and ten CNS chairs for the freaked out.

Somewhere in that maze, Dennis was sure to run across Oleo. There was no way of knowing if or when Oleo would arrive, so he did the only sensible thing: He waited for Oleo to find him.

Mary White had already arrived and was mingling in the main lounge, trying not to look too self-conscious. She sipped her drinks slowly, adept at remaining far behind the heavy drinkers and drug users, stretching her drinks while impatiently waiting for Dennis's angel to show.

He watched her move and handle herself in the crush of people and admired her grace, surprised at how easy and effortless she made it seem. She was still relatively young to have that much composure. Being born into a family with power, influence, and money, being exposed to this kind of life style, growing up with it, accepting it on a day to day basis, all showed. She was a child of the upper class and easily distinguished from the nouveaux riches.

She glanced in Dennis's direction and he smiled, hoping to bolster her confidence, reassure her, back up her frayed nerves. He had called her before he left the house and had explained that she would have to come to Bentwell's but was not to approach him under any conditions, at any time. He'd also told her to remain sober and straight, to wear something nice, and to leave the rest to him.

She'd done as he'd asked.

He guessed that, basically, beneath all those smooth, slick trappings and disguises, Mary was a nice person. It was a shame that Howard Warren—to hell with it. There was no sense thinking about him anymore.

Dennis did not want to mingle. He stood at the edges of the crowd as he usually did, red procurer's badge pinned to his shirt, watching. The people weren't the same tonight—there was something unsettling in his mood that made them seem threatening. Tinges of paranoia helped him keep his distance; he knew that by listening to his irrational fear he would be safer than if he ignored it. There was no harm in being safe.

He wiped his palms on his pants, brushing the small needle gun in his pocket for reassurance. After that call to Johnson, before he'd called Mary, he'd gone home and dug it out of his desk drawer, thinking it was better to be safe than sorry. You can't be too careful, he thought. His mouth and lips were dry, and a drink would have been nice to take the edge off, but he didn't relish the thought of walking through the crowd to get to the bar.

Mary was looking at him again. What was it with

her? Was she that curious about who her angel would be? It would go much better if she didn't look over once Oleo was by his side. She wouldn't scare him off—Dennis was certain of that—but it would be harder to discuss price and terms with Oleo once there was personal contact.

She was a commodity he was trying to sell, and the less personal it was, the easier it would go.

Maybe there was time to talk to her about it.

He pulled his hands out of his pockets and waited for her to look over again. He didn't have to wait long. He caught her attention and motioned for her to come over. She looked around quickly, as if trying to spot someone, then threaded her way through the crowd to his side. He grabbed her elbow firmly and swing her around so they weren't facing the crowd.

"What do you think you're doing out there?" he asked.

"What?"

"Stop looking over here every few seconds, will you? People are going to notice that—they'll think that something's going on, and I don't need that. We've got to keep a low profile or the whole deal's off." He glanced around the huge room, hoping to see Oleo's head above the crowd. "You don't want your parents to find out about this before it happens, do you?"

She shook her head, staring at the floor.

"Hey, take it easy. I didn't mean to jump on you like that. I just don't want you to look over at me anymore, okay? Just forget that I'm here. Have a good time."

She nodded again, then squeezed back into the mass of hot, sticky bodies.

She's going to blow it, he thought. This whole thing was a mistake. A bad mistake. I should have let her go to someone else. This isn't my kind of job.

He figured he really needed that drink, and he needed it enough to chance the walk to the bar. Besides, he couldn't spend the whole evening with his back to the wall. As he walked, though, he watched each person who bumped into him for a long moment, each pair of eyes, each set of lips, each pair of hands, waiting, looking for the gun, the knife, the injection. He made it to the bar.

Paranoia, he thought, sighing.

"Scotch and water," he told the bartender.

"Yes, sir, Mr. Lange."

His drink arrived quickly and he sat on a stool, back to the bar. There was no reason to be so jumpy. Nothing had happened, and nothing probably would. Nothing. The situation at home with Kira was doing strange things to his mind, putting more on edge than usual.

But, then again, Freddie had never before burst into heated anger like that. He'd lashed into Dennis for no apparent reason.

Dennis tasted the drink then shook his head, still unsure as to what, if anything, was going on.

"Something wrong with your drink?"

Dennis looked up, then up some more. It was Johnson, dressed in black, looking like a clumsy, too-meaty cat burglar. Dennis guessed the suit was very padded—it probably could have stuffed a mattress. "No, I was just thinking about something."

"What?" Oleo asked.

"It's not important. Let me buy you a drink."

Oleo nodded once, then ordered a vodka and tonic.

"She's here," Dennis said.

"Who's that?"

"My client."

"Oh."

Who did he think I was talking about? "I didn't want to talk about her over the phone. You've got to see her to believe the deal."

Oleo raised his eyebrows in disbelief. "Oh? Who is she?"

"Mary White." No sign of recognition, so Dennis continued. "She's Bill and Rose White's daughter. Heard of them?"

"Indeed," Oleo said. "Yes, indeed."

"Their little girl wants to get snuffed, but she doesn't want to get snuffed. Above all else, she doesn't want mommy or daddy to find out until afterwards."

"Don't they all," Oleo said, sipping his drink.

"She's young, and very unwilling. It seemed like a natural for you."

"Point her out."

Dennis pointed. "That's her. The one wearing the white wrap."

Oleo raised his eyebrows and pursed his lips in a silent whistle of appreciation. When he looked back at Dennis, he had a slightly crazed look in his eyes, like a hungry wolf looking at an unsuspecting animal. Dennis knew he had him.

"Just one problem," Dennis said, looking back at Mary.

"Besides her parents?"

Dennis laughed. "Don't worry about them. She's old enough to sign a release, and you can bet she will before anyone will lay a hand on her." He sipped his drink and swiveled around so he faced the bar. "She wants a lot of money. . . ."

"Don't worry about the money. I'm glad you thought of me. I've never liked her family, she's young and scared—it's perfect. I'd make her my victim on principle alone."

"You hate the Whites that much?"

"Well, a long time ago, they were investing a lot of money in the Centers. If they'd have used me as a broker, I would've been retired by now."

It didn't add up. There was something missing, some inner reason that Oleo was holding back. But that was Oleo's business—not Dennis's.

"Then you want her?"

Oleo smiled. "I certainly do. She's nice. Very nice."

"Fine. You want to discuss the fee now or later? It really doesn't matter. . . ."

"Later, then. I've got an appointment in a little while that I don't want to be late for." He gave Dennis a little wink.

"Okay. I'll be in touch."

"Yeah, fine. See you, Dennis."

Oleo walked through the crowd, his head high above almost every other person in the room. Mary White was by Dennis's side before Oleo got to the doors.

"That him?" she asked breathlessly.

"No."

"Who was he?"

"Listen, Mary—you're a nice kid and I like you, but don't press it, understand?"

She nodded. "When's he coming?"

"Soon. Didn't I tell you to stay over there? Go back and melt into the crowd. Have a good time and, with any luck, you'll be dead and reconstructed before you know it."

She didn't smile.

"Beat it," Freddie said to her. She looked into Freddie's eyes as if he were death incarnate, come to tap her on the shoulder with a finger of bone.

Dennis smiled at her expression. "Take off, Mary. This isn't him, either. I'll let you know."

She breathed a sigh and went back to the crowd.

"What's going on?" Freddie asked.

Dennis leaned back and stopped smiling. His expression grew hard and unreadable. "What do you want, Freddie?"

"Hey, relax! Take it easy!"

Dennis turned away from him and finished the scotch. Freddie tapped him on the shoulder.

"Leave me alone, Freddie. This is the way you want it, now don't you press your luck."

"I just wanted to apologize. I mean, there was no reason for me to blow up at you the way I did. I'm sorry. Most of it was Mara, you know? She eggs me on, burns my brain. I admit I got hot—maybe a little too hot, and stepped out of line. There was no call for that."

Dennis signed. "Another, bartender."

"Hey, come on! Loosen up a little, will you? Really. I mean, Mara's not even with me tonight. I left her home so she couldn't interfere or stop me from talking with you."

Dennis wheeled around and glared at him. "What do you want, Freddie? Huh? What is it? You want me to believe that Mara's got that much control over you? Is that it? Are you trying to tell me it's all her fault? If it was, how do I know this won't happen again tomorrow?"

Freddie nodded. "Sure, she's got a lot to do with it—hey, to hell with explanations. Why can't we be friends again?"

Friends again with Freddie Frank. An interesting concept and a dangerous proposition. Yet it was certainly superior to walking around having to glance over your shoulder all the time. Having to be suspicious was difficult and uncomfortable. It was like wearing shoes a half size too small. What the hell? Why not? Dennis grasped his hand and shook it.

"Let me buy you a drink," Freddie said.

"I'm fine," Dennis said, raising his glass.

"Things with Mara are pretty well shot."

"That's too bad," Dennis lied.

"How are things with you and Kira?"

"Better," Dennis said, nodding. "A lot better."

"Yeah? I didn't know that anything was wrong."

"Everything's fine."

"She sure is a beautiful woman. Beats Mara all to

hell. I even talked with her once—a couple of years ago, and I really liked her."

"I'll tell her that."

Freddie looked around the main lounge and made a face. "Say, why don't you and me move into one of the smaller lounges and talk? It's been a long time, you know? It'd be nice for a change."

Dennis shrugged. "Sure." He picked up his drink and followed Freddie. "Why not?"

Light, soft, gentle strains of music floated around them. A relaxing room, cozy, laid back, warmly decorated with wood paneling and several tastefully placed fireplaces. Dennis and Freddie found a corner table and sat, watching people interact, caress one another, trying to impress each other with their minds, their bodies, or their own very special trait. Dennis always enjoyed watching; he learned new techniques all the time and managed to put them to good use.

"What's with the girl?"

"Huh?"

"The girl. Out there," Freddie said, pointing to the main lounge. "What's with her?"

"A client of mine."

Freddie snorted a laugh. "How the hell you do it's beyond me."

Dennis smiled. "This one asked if she could be my client. I even tried talking her out of it."

Freddie shook his head. "You're really something else, Dennis, you know? Here I am, killing myself, working up a sweat, trying to come up with something totally different, something interesting, really amusing, and this girl just falls into your lap."

"What are you talking about?"

"The thing I'm working on?" He shrugged. "I've spent a lot of time and money on it—I hope to hell it works. If it does. . . ." He gestured with his hands.

"What's the gimmick?"

"No gimmick."

"Well what's it all about, then?" Dennis asked, curious both personally and professionally.

Freddie wagged a finger at him. "Oh, no you don't, Lange. You're welcome to come along and watch, to give an opinion or suggestion, but I'm not going to tell you anything about it. It wouldn't do the idea justice. It's very visual."

"That good?"

Freddie nodded. "Better."

"When's this thing supposed to take place?"

Freddie glanced at his watch. "In a little while." He frowned and lowered his glass to the table and rolled it slowly between his palms. "I'm not sure I should bring you along, though. I mean, we are in the same business, and we are competitors. But then again, we're friends, now. . . ."

"If you're worried about me trying something cute, I won't go. I don't need this feud starting up again."

Freddie took a few moments to study his drink and prepare an answer. He smiled, then said, "Come. I'd like you to be there. I can promise you it'll be everything I said it would be. And more."

Dennis nodded. "Great. Just let me tell Mary White I'm leaving."

"Is that who she is? Mary White?"

Dennis nodded. "That's her."

Freddie shook his head. "Some people have all the luck."

17

Paula Warren stood defiantly, fists resting on her ample hips, blocking the doorway. Her eyes radiated enough hatred to start a world war. "Who is she?" Paula asked. "Or is it a he?"

"Lay off," Warren spat. He finished smoothing back his wavy hair with his palms and looked away from the mirror.

She bobbed her head slowly, wisely, and screwed her face up in mock surprise. "Big man," she said. "You finally get to cut someone up. Planning on using a butter knife?"

"How I wish it was you," he mumbled.

"What?"

"I said that it was true. Tonight's the night."

"Yes, tonight's the night, all right. The night I leave. I never thought you'd really go through with it."

Warren laughed. "What the hell are you talking about, Paula? You think you know me? You think you can tell what I'm going to do all the time? What the hell do you know? What've you done, memorized my life?"

She shrank away from him as though he carried a contagious disease. He took a step closer and saw the fear in her eyes. It brought him to life; blood raced through his veins, pounded in his ears, drowning out most of her whimpering. He grabbed her by the shoulders and she screamed.

He let her go, and the coursing adrenaline left him feeling like an empty shell. "Good night, Paula. Don't wait up."

Paula sobbed her answer to the floor.

18

They took Dennis's car to the Center. Freddie was calm and relaxed, friendly, smiling and talking, all of which put Dennis off and took him by surprise. Dennis had to offer him a drink from his private stock, and Freddie graciously accepted. Dennis started to think that perhaps he'd been wrong about Freddie, that his original impression could have been the right one. If what Freddie was about to show him turned out to be half as good as he expected, then going into a partnership seemed a likely, mutually beneficial possibility.

"Tell me something about what's going to happen," Dennis said.

"Sorry, Dennis, but you'll just have to wait. Try to be patient. It may not work out right. If it doesn't, I'm going to need some feedback on what you've seen." Freddie wiped his forehead with the back of his hand. "Warm in here, isn't it?"

Dennis didn't think so; he shrugged and turned up the air conditioning unit.

"That's better. I want you to be able to relax and enjoy what you're about to see. I've reserved the entire bottom floor of the Center for our little experiment, so if anything goes wrong, we won't be bothered by outsiders."

Dennis nodded. "That takes a considerable amount of money. Who's backing this?"

Freddie smiled and shook his head. "No names. It's a joint venture."

Dennis shrugged and looked out the car window. It was one thing to be close-mouthed about a venture that could bring in a lot of money, but it was something else entirely to stay absolutely quiet around another professional. Maybe it wasn't entirely legal. If what Freddie had in mind was illegal, then that could easily explain his silence. But it wouldn't explain why he would want Dennis as a witness. He was glad he had the needle gun—just as a precaution.

"Nice night," Freddie said.

"Yeah. Nice."

Freddie sat in the private viewing booth, smiling, excited, and very anxious to have everything work out. Dennis sat beside him, enjoying his nervousness. Dennis had seen no other people in the hallways, and all of the white rooms were empty. So far, Freddie was keeping his word.

None of the other viewing booths were occupied; Freddie had gotten a package deal from the Center and had rented them all.

He watched Freddie glance at his watch, lick his lips, glance at his watch again, then peer through the booth's transparent wall, the wall facing the small white room. The booth's outer wall was made of the same material as the white room's outer wall, and was virtually unbreakable. Within the white room sat the bed; the only necessary piece of furniture. Freddie glanced at his watch again.

"Well?" Dennis asked, egging Freddie on, amused by his jerky movements.

"I don't know—they should have started by

now." He looked harried, concerned, as though each moment something wasn't happening cost him a small fortune.

"When was it supposed to start?"

"A few minutes ago." Freddie started slapping his thigh with his riding crop.

"Want me to check on things for you? See what's holding them up?" Dennis offered.

"No! I'll do it. Sit tight, okay? I'll be right back."

"Okay."

Freddie stood and opened the door to the booth. He glanced back at Dennis, still holding the door open, and shook his head. "Too bad."

"What's that?"

The door closed, the lock clicked, and Freddie stood outside the booth, looking in through the wall. "Too bad," he said again, shaking his head. His voice sounded tinny through the wall speaker. "Too bad you couldn't have left me alone. I thought the whole matter over carefully, and I decided that you'd probably prefer to watch this alone. I will be right next door, though, in the next booth. I'll be watching, too."

He turned his back on Dennis.

"All right, Mara. Now."

The door in the back wall of the white room opened and Mara walked in smiling, as though she had an audience of thousands. She looked directly into Dennis's eyes, seemed amused by his confusion and appprehensive expression, then looked at Freddie. "Can you hear me all right?" she asked.

Dennis nodded.

"Yes," Freddie said.

"Is his door locked?" Mara asked.

"Of course it's locked! What do you take me for, an idiot?" Freddie demanded.

She looked like she was about to say something, then smiled and turned quickly away. She went back through the rear door. She re-entered, leading a hooded woman. She sat her down on the edge of the bed, then went out through the front and entered the next booth with Freddie.

"What the hell's going on?" Dennis asked.

No one answered.

"Freddie?"

Nothing.

He got up to leave and pressed on the booth's door. It was locked. The woman sitting in the white room swayed in the rhythms of someone caught in the throes of dust—an addict's ecstasy. Euphoric beyond comprehension.

Two men were walking down the narrow hallway, approaching from the left. Despite the fact that they were hooded, Dennis was certain the taller man was Oleo Johnson. Dennis had no idea as to who the other man was. They walked calmly, as though they were out for a stroll through the park on a nice summer day.

What the hell was going on? What is this? he thought.

The two men nodded to Freddie's booth, then to Dennis, then walked boldly into the white room. Johnson walked right by the hooded woman and opened the rear door, reached around the wall, and picked up a jar. He shook it, then placed it on the floor by the head of the bed. He closed the rear door.

"All right. Lock it up," Oleo's muffled voice said.

Dennis heard the locks click. He sat back down in the booth's chair.

The shorter man pulled off his hood.

Howard Warren.

Oleo did the same, then gestured toward the woman. "After you," he said.

Warren leered, took a step closer, then struck the dust addict with the back of his hand.

"You call that a slap?" Oleo asked.

Warren slapped her again, only harder. The crack

116

of contact rang through the viewing booth. Dennis's palms started to sweat. He'd seen Oleo work only once. And once was enough. Coming along on this ridiculous trip was a mistake. He wanted to leave.

"Unlock the door, Freddie," Dennis said calmly but forcefully.

No response.

"Freddie?"

Nothing.

"Mara?"

Still nothing.

Oleo had stripped the woman of her clothes and, through the dim lighting, Dennis couldn't see much detail. She looked to be in excellent condition for an addict, though. Oleo started slapping her breasts and thighs. After a few moments, angry red welts covered the slapped portions of her skin. The woman swayed, locked into her dust dreams.

"Come on you guys. I'm falling asleep," Mara said. Freddie chuckled.

Oleo stripped down and Howard Warren kneeled on her shoulders, pinning her to the mattress.

Mara shouted words of encouragement as Oleo pumped away. With each thrust, Warren slapped and gouged her already raw skin.

Then it was Warren's turn. He lubricated himself, turned the woman over, and rammed into her.

She screamed in pain.

Dennis froze, eyes wide, mouth open, cold sweat dotting his body, silently echoing her scream. It was Kira.

"Kira!"

Warren pumped for all he was worth.

"Kira!"

He pounded on the transparent wall, kicked at the door till his feet throbbed in pain, till his hands were bloody. She lay motionless on the mattress.

Oleo withdrew a straight-edge razor and held it

117

up to the soft light, letting the rays glint off its polished, honed surface, off his gleaming eyes.

Dennis backed up as far as he could and threw himself at the door.

Oleo turned her over onto her back again. He started a careful, neat, shallow incision beginning at her collarbone and ending right below the tip of her sternum. A thin red line followed the razor's path.

"Skin," Oleo said. "I like skin."

Warren nodded, looking a little peaked.

"What's the matter?" Oleo asked him.

"Nuh—nothing." He forced himself to bend over and kiss the blood away from between Kira's breasts.

Dennis threw himself at the door again.

"Kira!"

Warren played with the blood as though he were finger painting.

Dennis threw himself at the booth's transparent wall but bounced off, landing on the floor. He clutched his shoulder. It was Kira in there. Kira.

My Kira.

My Kira.

He cried.

He got to his knees, used the chair for support, and made it back onto the seat. He saw Oleo through salty tears. Oleo was pouring the liquid from the jar all over her body. He and Warren grabbed her and lifted her from the bed, leaned her against the room's clear front wall so she faced Dennis. Oleo ripped off her hood.

The dust showed in her eyes, but not enough to hide or mask the terror, the pain, the horror, the humiliation.

Warren left the room.

Oleo stood in the doorway.

She saw Dennis then, recognized him, and silently mouthed his name. Dennis saw, knew she was aware, and threw himself at the front of the booth again and again.

She whispered Dennis's name through her pain.

Then Oleo threw the lit match.

Like a dead, dried-out tree in the middle of a raging forest fire, like a pack of matches tossed into a roaring furnace, like a meteorite plunging through the Earth's atmosphere, like a sun gone nova, she burned. And burned. And burned.

And burned.

19

Freddie Frank liked the way Dennis looked, lying there on the floor of the viewing booth, unconscious. It was the way the plan had worked, the way Dennis hadn't even suspected a thing that made him swell with pride like an overripe melon. He pocketed the needle gun and stood in the doorway, smiling.

"Come on, Freddie. We've got things to take care of," Mara said from the hallway.

"Take it easy. There's no rush," Freddie said, still staring at Dennis.

It was nice to think of Dennis as being dead rather than stunned. It allowed Freddie's imagination to run wild, to taste the money and power that would soon be his. There was no need to run out of the Center like a common criminal. After all, Kira would be reconstructed—no one had harmed her crystal.

Freddie felt something on his shoulder and turned. "Hey, Oleo."

Oleo narrowed his smile, tightened his lips, and lost the glint in his eyes. "Everything all right?"

Freddie nodded. "Just fine."

"I'm glad to hear that."

"I think we taught him a lesson."

"We?" Oleo asked.

Freddie shrugged, then smiled. "All right, all right. No need to get huffy."

"Let's get *out* of here," Mara said. "This place is giving me the creeps."

"Yeah, okay," Freddie reluctantly agreed.

Oleo stepped in front of Freddie, blocking his path. "Aren't you forgetting something?"

"Forgetting something?" He turned to Mara. "Are we forgetting anything, dear?"

She shook her head. "Not that I can remember."

Oleo sneered and reached forward, grabbing two handfuls of Freddie's polo shirt. He lifted him a few centimeters to make sure Freddie got the message.

"Relax, Johnson. Relax. He's right in there," Freddie said, pointing to a white room ten meters away.

Oleo strode over to the clear outer wall and peered through. A smile spread across his face and, as he turned to look at Freddie and Mara, he gave them the "thumbs up" signal. "That's more like it."

Freddie smiled back. "I told you it would be mutually beneficial."

Oleo walked into the room. Howard Warren drifted over and glanced through the wall. "Who's that?"

"A gentleman named Berkman. George Berkman," Mara said.

"Who?" Warren asked.

"It's not important, Warren. Don't worry yourself about it."

But Warren was transfixed before the clear wall, staring in rapt admiration for Oleo's work. At least he's watching one of the best, Freddie thought. One of the very best.

"They'll be all right. Can we get out of here, now?" Mara asked.

"Sure." He smiled and sighed. "It was a good night, you know?"

Mara shook her head and stared at Freddie. "It may have been for you. You didn't have to cop the dust. You didn't have to pin her down to inject her. You didn't have to drag her out to the car. You didn't have to—"

"Let it alone, Mara."

"Let it alone, Mara," she mimicked.

Freddie wheeled, and swung his riding crop at her bare midriff with all his might, but missed. She'd moved out of range. Freddie saw that she was getting better at anticipating his moods. He didn't feel like advancing on her to ensure another blow landed—he had made his point.

But she had made hers, too.

She would never let him forget. Never. Just by being alive, she would serve as a constant reminder, a constant source of nagging irritation. He realized the bounds of his mistake, and regretted having agreed to her plan. And it had been her plan. It had been her plan all along.

She had suggested they get Johnson and Warren to do in Kira. She had suggested that Dennis be forced to witness the whole thing. She had arranged for the rooms at the Center. She had worked out all the details, all the paperwork. She had dragged Kira from the house out into the car and then to the Center.

She, she, she.

Freddie glanced at her and, for the first time since he'd known her, thought he understood the distant expression on her face. She was a planner, a devious, dangerous combination of deep cunning within and fixed determination without. He knew he would never feel safe again, could never let his guard down and relax, even for a moment. She would always be there, right over his shoulder, watching, waiting, planning, making it clear who was in control, who had managed to edge Dennis Lange out of the business.

She had ... well, it really wasn't the killer instinct, he thought, but it was something close to that. Freddie would have been happier if Dennis were dead—just to be rid of him once and for all. He remembered the way her eyes had come to life when she'd talked about her plan. Killing wouldn't solve a thing, she had said.

But torture would.

Kill Lange, and Kira will have him reconstructed, she'd explained. After all, Dennis had a crystal, and as long as Kira could produce it, Dennis could come back to life. He wouldn't remember who had killed him or how he'd been killed, but it wouldn't have taken him long to find out. And once he found out, neither Freddie nor Mara would have ever been safe.

But if they killed Kira Dennis would have to understand and face the fact that they meant business. He would back off and give Freddie some breathing room. He might even quit the business. Kira would be none the worse for the whole thing, since she would remember nothing of what had happened to her after her last crystal update.

Sure. Mara had worked out the whole thing. And Freddie realized he'd been stupid enough to let her. Or had it been stupid? At least now he knew something about Mara he might never have known until it was too late. He nodded as they walked through the narrow hallway.

But the whole plan still relied on too many ifs. There was no way of predicting just how Dennis would react, just which way he would go. It would have been much simpler if they'd smashed Dennis's crystal before the Center could use it. Then Lange would be dead. Permanently.

But then there would have been an investigation, most probably. And an investigation meant police.

She had told him that. She had.

She, she, she.

Freddie smiled at her as the door opened to let

them get to the parking lot. He could see by her reaction that his smile was getting better. Perhaps all it took was time and practice, he thought. He was afraid he was going to have to kill her, and developing a good smile would be necessary to put her at ease, to get her to relax, to get her to trust him more.

And she could no longer be trusted.

But then again, neither could Johnson nor Warren. They both knew too much, had seen too much. Freddie sighed. He was going to be very busy.

20

Dennis came out of the fog of unconsciousness slowly, like a diver decompressing on his way up from the murky depths. He looked for memories, facts, landmarks which might serve as orientative aids as he fought to place his surroundings. Slowly at first, then all in a rush, his memories flooded back.

Kira.

He sat up in bed quickly and glanced around the room. He was in a Center. But they hadn't killed him. They hadn't killed him and he wasn't reconstructed. He couldn't have been reconstructed—he wouldn't have remembered what those ... those bastards had done to Kira. And that had been their mistake. They should have left Kira alone.

Kira.

Where was she now? In the basement of the Center being reconstructed? Caught somewhere between life and death? Or had they destroyed her crystal, too? He realized that she might not be taken care of properly. The Center might not have retrieved her crystal or, worse, Frank might have really done something to it. What time was it? What *day* was it?

He leapt out of bed and searched the room quickly with his eyes, looking for a door which might lead to a closet. A man entered without knocking. He was dressed in white, was a little taller than Dennis, and looked meaty, the kind of build usually found on weightlifters. He moved across the room smoothly, effortlessly, his movements belying his muscle-bound appearance, and stood by Dennis's side.

"Where are my clothes?" Dennis asked.

"Right in there, Mr. Lange," he said, motioning toward a nearby door. "You're feeling all right, then?"

"No, I'm not feeling all right," he said, measuring and weighing his words, aiming them at the man as though each word were a bullet. "Please step aside— I've got to get dressed."

The man in white smiled. "If you're not feeling well, perhaps it would be best if you stayed in bed for the rest of the day."

Rest of the day? "How long have I been here?" Dennis demanded.

"Two days."

"Two days? Are you kidding?"

The man in white shook his head. "We all found it very strange—shock was not the expected reaction, but everything seems to check out fine, now."

"What the hell are you talking about?"

"Shock. You went into a state of shock, and we had no other choice but to treat you for it."

"Kira. My wife. How is she?"

The man nodded. "Oh, she's fine. Relax, now, Mr. Lange. Everything has been handled just as you specified. Would you like to get back into bed, now?"

"What the hell are you talking about?" Dennis yelled. The man was about to repeat his request, but Dennis silenced him with a wave of his hand. "Where did you say my clothes were?"

"Right in there. Then you're feeling better, now?"

Dennis pulled his clothes out of the closet with enough force and power to have ripped the door off. He started dressing. "I feel great. Never felt better."

"You don't sound it."

Dennis froze, one arm halfway through his shirt sleeve. "What's that supposed to mean? What's the matter? How the hell did you expect me to act after ... after that atrocity?"

The man in white looked confused.

"Never mind. What's your job?"

"I'm a nurse," the man answered indignantly.

"Jesus Christ. A nurse." He shook his head and finished dressing.

Two days. Two whole terrible days with Kira lying on a cold slab in the corner of the sub-basement while he slept comfortably in the Center's bed. Two whole terrifying days for Freddie and Mara Frank to run around loose and tie up loose ends, to cause more trouble, to make plans, while he was under sedation.

He pushed the nurse aside and stormed out into the hall. Nothing looked familiar. He'd never been on this floor before. He'd never had to. Through his job, he was familiar with the two lower floors. He had to be on at least the third or fourth—that was where the hospital rooms were located. But he didn't know anyone from that area—all his contacts were downstairs.

He walked through the halls briskly, ignoring the inner voice that told him speed no longer mattered. He found the tube, tapped his foot in a rapid, irregular rhythm while he waited for the capsule, then rode it to the ground with his finger pressed firmly and constantly on the button marked "Lobby."

The capsule stopped, the door slid upward, and he walked onto the cushiony floor. Chimes sounded high overhead, people rushed back and forth madly, lines queued up in front of booths and counters. . . . Where now? What next?

And he stopped, realizing that he'd never had to do this before, that although he had a general idea as to what had to be done, he had no idea how to go about it.

Freddie Frank. That bastard. He had to be insane. There was no way he could expect to get away with this. What was the point? Could Freddie really hate anyone so much? Could that much greed fester and explode in any human being?

"May I help you, sir?" a woman asked. She was smiling, standing before him. She was small—smaller than Kira, but her hair was light blonde and about Kira's length. She looked very young.

"Yes, uhm . . ." and Dennis fought for the words to explain just what it was that he wanted, just what had happened.

"Sir?"

He started to explain the whole thing to her. She would understand. It would be necessary for her to help him set everything straight. Then it all came out—but it came out so quickly—Freddie and Mara, Oleo and Warren, the way they'd used her, doped her up, beaten her, Freddie and Mara, Johnson and Howard, the way they'd beaten her, cut her, the sick, sick torture—

"Sir?"

—the way they calmly coated her with something that made her burn, and burn, and burn—

"Hey, are you okay?" the woman asked.

He looked up at her, realizing he was on his knees and shaking uncontrollably.

"Sir?"

He told her he was okay, that it was getting chilly in the lobby, that they should turn down the cold air blasting him, that Kira had seen and recognized him and had spoken his name through her burning lips, that she hadn't done anything to deserve—

"Don't move!" the woman ordered.

He told her he was fine and she shouldn't worry about him, that it was Kira who needed help, that every moment he waited made it that much more complicated for the reconstruction technicians. They would have to work fast—

And then he realized he hadn't been talking, that he was lying on the floor curled in a fetal position, shivering, shaking. Two men picked him up and carried him.

He screamed. And screamed.

And screamed.

21

Kira sat up in bed, eyes open, mind suddenly alert and aware. She was surrounded by unfamiliar objects, strange colors and shapes, a room she had never seen; she fought off the rapidly rising panic. Fear snaked its way through her system, then settled, coiled in her stomach.

Something had happened. Where was Dennis?

Dennis.

"Dennis?" she shouted.

No answer. The mint-green walls absorbed the cry, holding his name, not letting it reach him on the other side.

And then she realized where she was.

Recognition came to her like a sickness, emptying her of strength, of hope. The poison of adrenaline hit her hard, caused her to shake, to tremble. She doubled over, grabbed the edge of the bed, and fought back the urge to vomit. She sat on the bed and stared at the friendly patterns the tile made on the floor, the nice paintings hanging on the inoffensive walls, the walls' serene color and texture, the logical calm arrangement of furniture—she wanted to scream.

Reconstructed.

She started to cry.

Reconstructed.

She felt something inside falling, slipping away from the room, from the Center, from her emotions. She was empty, her feelings blocked, unable to guide her reactions; she fought to gain control of herself and to force herself to accept what had happened. It was as though she were a different person, watching a woman sitting on the edge of a bed, crying hysterically.

She stopped crying.

She was reconstructed.

Reconstructed.

The word seemed cruel, mechanical, without tenderness or humanity or understanding. Reconstruction is what happens to an automobile after an accident, a computer after it fries, a holowall after the support poles collapse—not to a human being. People aren't rebuilt, renovated, redecorated.

She giggled, sniffling, wiping at the wet trails the tears had left on her cheeks. Just like the car, Kira thought. Traded in for a younger, newer model.

Reconstructed.

She found it funny, absurd, and laughed uncontrollably. Her sides hurt, her stomach started to cramp in pain, and she fought for breath. It was ridiculous. Reconstructed.

And then she realized she was sobbing wildly, madly, unable to stop.

She came back to herself slowly, gradually, in stages. Reason returned, reinforced by pain and hurt—her newly accepted reality. She was alive, physically younger by about five years, but with no idea as to how much was missing from her memory. She would have a better idea as soon as she found out when she had ... died.

She was almost getting used to the idea.

She didn't particularly like it, but she knew she had no other choice but to accept it. The counselor had helped her adjust for the short time he had spent with her. His attitude had been confusing, though, and Kira had been disturbed by it. Still, she wasn't sure how much of her perceptions she could trust. Things were different, now. Very different.

The counselor had refused to discuss Dennis with her. He had told her that his main intention was to get her calmed down and as rational as possible. He'd said that he or another counselor would return later, when she had a grip on her emotions and had accepted what she was. Then they would talk. He couldn't understand why she asked so many questions about what had happened. He seemed surprised, as if she were the only person who had ever acted that way.

Kira shrugged, shook her head, then paced around the room. The floor was cold beneath her bare feet, the walls were too close, the furniture got in the way. She would run her hands over her face every few minutes to find the creases around her eyes gone, her skin fresh and smooth.

Why weren't they telling her what had happened? They either thought she already knew about it, or were hiding it from her for some reason, or they didn't know, themselves. She wished Dennis was with her.

The counselor had been purposely vague on Dennis's whereabouts, and she was becoming suspicious. He should have gotten her out by now, unless ... unless he'd been reconstructed, too. But the counselor would have told her that.

She needed to smash something, throw something, scream, hurl a vase of flowers through the wall, rip the stuffing out of the mattress. Her fingernails dug into her palms. She squeezed her eyes shut with all her might and held her breath, choking back a scream.

The tears started to flow again, slowly, with an

almost peaceful serenity. They dropped unheaded to the sheets.

"Hi," the woman said. Her voice was light, full of happiness and optimism. She stood in the doorway, clipboard under an arm, smiling. She was a little taller than Kira, about ten years older, and radiated a sense of security and self assurance. "My name's Norma."

Kira nodded to her. "Hello."

"How are you feeling?"

"Well enough."

"Well enough to talk?"

Norma's smile seemed infectious, and Kira felt herself come back a little more. She found herself not wanting to talk to the woman, yet trusting her for no apparent reason. "What about?" Kira asked.

"About you. We've—well, I'm an orientation counselor. I had a talk with Dr. Childs—"

"Who?"

"Dr. Childs. The man you talked to earlier today. He asked me to drop by and see you to make sure you're okay."

"I'm okay."

"Why don't we take a walk, then? There are some things I'd like to show you."

"All right," Kira said. She was wary, unsure of what Norma had in mind, and not at all interested in a guided tour. She resolved not to say anything, though, until she got some answers. But she still got off the bed and followed Norma out of the room and into the hall.

"Dr. Childs said you were very disoriented when you came out of it," Norma said as they walked.

"I was. And I still am. What happened?"

Norma slowed, then stopped, casually glancing at Kira's eyes. "What do you mean?"

"I want to know what happened to me. How did I die? Where's my husband? Why isn't he with me?"

"Oh." Norma's face was a blank, a carefully con-

133

structed mask designed to hide the analytical process that was going on in her mind. "Were you reconstructed without a ... no, that's impossible, given your mental state. When was the last time you had your crystal updated?"

Kira shrugged. "A while ago, I guess. I don't even know how long I've been here. If you tell me that, I might be able to tell you when."

Norma nodded. "I see. Listen, Kira, the walk can wait. Let's go to my office. There are some things you should know."

Kira nodded once. "I agree."

Norma smiled and put a friendly, matronly arm around Kira's shoulders. "You know, I don't really have any solid information about you, about your relationship with your ... husband. Would you mind talking to me about some of these things?"

"No," Kira said.

"Good."

Norma's office was decorated with gay colors, the walls lined with bookcases and curios, small souvenirs and knickknacks that were more sentimental than beautiful. Kira found the office both cozy and comfortable—a pleasant and distinct change from the somber antiseptic hallways and the sterile cold room she had woken up in.

There was a short sofa in the office, a coffee table before it, and two chairs on either side of the table. The arrangement reminded Kira of her own living room, and her breath came more easily as her muscles relaxed a little. Norma had offered Kira some coffee, and Kira had accepted gladly. Norma sat on the sofa while Kira sat on the chair to her left.

There had been no tests, no word association games, no puzzles to take apart and put together. Norma laughed, joked and put Kira at ease, gradually asking questions. She got Kira to talk about herself until the problems and fears flowed out of their own volition. The years poured out, and Norma was kind, perceptive, and genuinely interested.

When Kira had finished, Norma looked very confused.

"Are you sure you're telling me everything? Even about your sexual preferences?"

Kira nodded. "Yes."

"And that's as far as you remember? Talking to this man, this potential angel of your husband's?"

"Yes. Howard Warren."

"Right. Howard Warren. Well, if I'm going to tell you what happened after that phone call, you've got to promise me something."

"What?"

"You've got to let me help you deal with it. From what you've told me, your actions leading up to your death are going to be difficult for you to accept."

What had happened? Kira wondered. "Fine. I'd appreciate it, Norma. It sounds pretty bad."

Norma smiled and sighed. "Bad? I don't know. It depends on how you look at it. You can make this hard or easy. It's all up to you."

"I understand."

"Fine, then. There appears to have been a definite reconciliation between you and Dennis. Now, either this reconciliation was based upon your becoming a client for him, or it worked out that way after the reconciliation. You could have agreed on it to spice up the sexual side of your marriage."

"*Client?*"

"Yes. You signed a release form and went into a white room with two men—two of your husband's angels. Your husband and two of his associates watched the whole thing from the privacy of a viewing booth."

"No!" she yelled, shaking her head violently.

Norma said nothing.

Kira jumped to her feet, hands balled into fists by the side of her head, tears streaming down her cheeks,

heart pounding; the illness in her stomach had returned. A sound from deep inside, an animal-like
whimper buried under years of suppression, a maniacal scream that was the border between the conscious
and the unconscious, rose slowly, burrowing its way
upward through the layers of personality until it
erupted, spewing forth a denial that no one could ever
contend.

Norma was by her side, holding her, trying to
calm her.

"*No*," Kira whined in a tortured voice. "I won't
believe it! It's not true!"

Norma hugged her shoulders to try to transfer
some of her own strength to Kira. "I'm afraid it is,
Kira. I'm afraid it is."

22

Dr. Childs' office was the epitome of what Dennis had always thought a psychologist's office would look like. Busts of pioneers in the field of psychiatry sat on dustless shelves; paintings straight from the id hung on the calm walls; innocuous music without melody or life clutterd the air; books and journals were neatly arranged in size and numerical order in the polished bookcases.

"Well, Mr. Lange, it's certainly good to see you up and around. Feeling better?"

Dennis nodded.

"That was quite an adverse reaction you had."

Dennis nodded again.

"Do you still intend to go to the police with this story of yours?"

"Yes," Dennis said. "I remember what happened, doctor. I was there—you weren't. I know Freddie and Mara Frank—you don't."

Dr. Childs shrugged. "Well, it's certainly your prerogative. But keep in mind that all the release forms were signed, the applications for the rooms had your name—"

"On them. It's enough," he said, holding up his hands. "We've already been through this twice. There is absolutely no need to go through it again."

"Very well, then. What are your future plans?"

"I want to see my wife."

"Under the law, she is no longer your wife, Mr. Lange. And she does not wish to see you at this time."

"I don't care. I still want to see her."

"Why? Why this compulsion? What is it you plan to say to her? What magic words do you intend to use? What phrase you utter will erase what you've done to her? What's going on inside your head?"

"Fuck off, Doctor. I'm not interested."

Childs shook his head and breathed a deep heavy sigh. "You're not letting me help you."

"You don't want to help me—all you want to do is cure me. Whether I'm sick or not."

Childs leaned back in his chair and smiled disarmingly. "Very well, then, Mr. Lange. You may see your wife."

"When?"

"Soon enough. In a few moments, if you wish. There are, however, a few points which you should be made aware of before you do see her. She's been under the care of a very good counselor. Dr. Norma Lynn is of the opinion that your wife is not ready to see you. It's too soon for her—too close to her reconstruction. And I happen to feel that it's too soon for *you.*

"Your wife is not capable of dealing with her emotions or with you at the present time. Perhaps in a few days she'll be better . . . more capable of handling the emotional turmoil seeing you would undoubtably bring about. She was told the circumstances surrounding her death only a few hours ago. If you still insist on seeing her now, we won't stop you."

"But."

"She has had a tremendous shock. And you, Mr. Lange, are at the root of her shock."

"Right. You said I could see her now?"

Childs shrugged. "She's right through that door," he said, pointing to his left.

Dennis licked his dry lips and wiped the beads of sweat off his palms onto his pants legs. He slapped his knees lightly in standing and stared at a flower on Childs's shirt.

This was it. They couldn't keep him from her any longer. She was alive again, and no matter what they tried to tell him, *he* knew what had happened, and nothing would ever change that. He would explain it to her, and she would listen. She would have to listen. They would go home together and work out their problems just as they had done once before. No matter what they told Kira, no matter what lies Childs and Lynn believed, there was still a chance of working it out.

Dennis knew that Frank was behind the whole thing—but he also knew that Frank didn't have the money to pull off anything as elaborate as this. He couldn't have bought two doctors; Childs and Lynn actually must believe Freddie's setup. They did have all the papers—signed, witnessed, and authenticated by the Administration Complex; there was no reason why they should believe Dennis's story over the one the facts pointed to.

Freddie had been extremely thorough.

Perhaps too thorough to have done it by himself.

"I see you're having second thoughts," Childs said.

"No, not at all," Dennis said. He started walking toward the door. "I do want to thank you, though. I mean it. You really have helped, even though it wasn't in the way you wanted to."

Dennis grasped the door handle. It was cold to the touch. He swung the door open and walked into the room.

She was there. Kira. Younger, cuter, pert and very nervous. She'd been startled by the sound of the door opening, and sat totally still, like a deer transfixed with fear. She stared into his eyes, searching, pleading, imploring, demanding he tell her that none of it was true, that Norma had been wrong, that the records and papers were misleading, that they lied. He started to smile at her and the spark of love that was Kira left; her eyes glassed over with defenses and her mouth was transformed into a cool, noncommittal smile. The smile of a stranger.

He let go of the door handle and pulled it shut behind him. "Hi," he said. He felt as if every word he spoke, every action he made, every breath he took, was being watched by millions on their holowalls to be studied and analyzed.

"Hi," she said to him.

She was afraid. He could tell. It was awkward, and quickly getting worse. The difficulty in bridging the gap increased geometrically with each passing second, with each heartbeat, and he felt himself weaken, give up, to let her draw whatever conclusions she wished. He was tired of fighting them all. He sank into the chair opposite hers and rubbed his face with his hands. He wanted to try, though, and considered smiling. But he ruled that out immediately; she knew his smile for what it was. This was no time for lies. This was no time for deception. This was no time for manipulation.

"Doctor Lynn told me what happened to you, Dennis. About the breakdown, I mean."

He nodded. "I'm better now, baby. Much better. It was too much for me to cope with and I guess I just fell apart. I didn't think something like that could ever happen to me. I'm sorry it did. It shouldn't have. If I'd kept myself under control, we both could have been out of here by now."

She looked away, to the wall on her right. He followed her line of sight; she was looking at a still life, a bowl of fruit. Ridiculous. He looked back at her; she still stared at the painting.

"You believe them, don't you," he said, hurting over each word, pulling them out into the open so he had to face them along with her.

"No, I don't think so. At least I'm not as sure about what happened as they are." She looked back at him, leaned forward so she was nearer, and lowered her voice as if they might be overheard. "They don't know you, Dennis. Being married is about as kinky as you'll ever get. It's certainly kinky enough for me. You wouldn't have wanted to do that to me. You wouldn't even let me do it if I begged you to let me go into that room. And even if you did somehow get me to do it, I can't believe you would want to watch.

"It's not as though we hated each other, or we didn't love each other. I mean, we have our differences, our problems, and maybe we do fight a lot, but I don't believe it could ever have been bad enough for you to . . . to. . . ."

"Yeah, I know," he said heavily. She leaned closer and took his hands in hers. "I love you, Kira."

"I love you, too."

He looked up from the floor, into her green deep eyes. "Would you like to get out of here? Do you want to go home?"

She looked at his knees. "Home," she said slowly, as if trying to remember what the word meant, where she had heard it before. "They're not going to let us go home. Even if we both agreed to stay married, they still wouldn't let us go home. A 'readjustment period,' Dr. Lynn called it. She explained the whole thing to me."

"Okay," he said, swallowing with difficulty. "Not home, then. Anywhere. You name it."

"I don't know."

"Then I'll choose."

"No, that's not what I meant."

"Then you don't believe me. You think that I let

those two—two—animals use you like that and sat through the whole thing for my amusement?"

"No, it's not like that. I meant what I said about the snuff. I really did."

"What was it, then?"

She sighed and let go of his hands. She sat back and held onto the arms of her chair as if deriving some strength from them. "It's us. You and me. We're no good for each other. We fight all the time. We don't even have fun anymore. Living together is a slow torture."

"Don't talk to me about torture," he said bitterly.

She looked surprised, taken aback. "I'm sorry. That came out wrong. I didn't mean to say that, but you've got to see what I mean. It's just no good with us. I was, well—I was thinking about splitting up before this even happened."

"I know. I was, too. But we resolved all that."

Her eyebrows rose and her lips parted.

"We did."

She said nothing.

"I tell you, we settled all our differences."

"Then there was a reconciliation?"

"Yes," he said. "There was."

"When?"

"A day before you died. Listen, Kira, none of this is really that important right now. I love you, and I need you. I want us to go on. Together. Nothing's changed for me."

She said nothing. He waited while she thought it over. He was afraid to say anything else, for fear of alienating her or pushing her into a decision. But he also wanted and needed to say more, to tell her how strongly he felt, to explain the pain and the hurt and the suffering he felt deep inside. He was about to take that chance when she spoke.

"No."

And that was it. His chest hurt and felt empty at the same time; his vision started to blur. He wiped the tears away with the back of his hand. She looked at him and realized what he thought, that he'd misunderstood. She jumped from her chair and bounded across the two meters separating them, throwing her arms around his neck.

"No. No, I'm not going to let anyone do this to us. We'll stay together," she said. "We'll try again." She loosened her grip for a moment. "But on a trial basis."

He hugged her. Ten day trial. That would be time enough. He would have to set the relationship straight. Nothing else would interfere. He would let nothing get in the way of having Kira back.

She could have sent him away. He knew that was her legal right; they were no longer legally married after her reconstruction.

A ten day trial.

And at the end of that time, Kira would have to decide whether she wanted to stay, or to go.

They cried together.

But festering deep inside him, like a cancer growing at a tremendous rate, was a hatred like none he'd ever felt before. And at the pit of the hate sat an image: Freddie and Mara and Oleo and Howard, all crumpled heaps of agonized flesh. And all very, very dead.

But Kira couldn't know. She wouldn't know. He would not tell her his dream, his desire, his need, his hatred—there would be problems enough without having her involved in his retribution.

23

The hot night air settled on the city in a smothering embrace. Dennis knew she was watching him, staring at his back through the glass door, studying his movements, hoping that, somehow, that would set her mind at ease. The air was stuffy, difficult to breathe, and yet he didn't want to go back into the living room. Not yet.

Two hundred meters below the balcony, on the Avenida del Fuego, points of light snaked through the street despite the unseasonable heat. Tourists, crammed into tiny electric cars linked together like segments of a worm, listened to tinny electric guides describe Mexico City's night spots. He was glad he wasn't down there with them, but he was close to wishing he wasn't alone in the hotel suite with Kira.

Kira.

He turned around and looked into the room. She had been staring at him, just as he'd thought. Her movements were jerky, awkward, as she tried to cover up being caught in the act. He sighed and shook his head, afraid that coming here had been a mistake, that the relationship was dead, that nothing would really work, that he had already lost her. He watched her fix a drink at the bar.

His sides were soaked with sweat. Rivulets of perspiration dripped down inside his shirt and collected around the band of his pants. Staying out on the balcony any longer would be masochistic; he had to go back in. He hesitated a moment, hand on the door, then took a deep breath and pulled it open.

He was hit by a chilling blast of air.

"It's hot out there," he said, closing the door behind him. She sat down on the suspensor couch.

"Oh? I thought you might be taking a sauna."

He laughed without humor. "It was almost that bad." He walked over to the bar and fixed himself a mescanol. Kira crossed her legs and sipped at her drink, staring into space, daydreaming, seeing nothing.

Dennis stirred his drink with a swizzle stick. "What would you like to do tomorrow?" he asked.

"What? I'm sorry—I wasn't listening."

"I just wanted to know if you had any special plans for tomorrow. Do you want to go anyplace? There's a lot to see here. And a lot to do."

She shrugged and took a sip. "I don't know."

He crossed the room and sat in a chair beside the couch. "Well, we ought to do something."

"We are."

He sighed. "No, something different. Something really special. Maybe go to the casino."

She shrugged again.

"How about visiting the cathedrals?"

She made a face.

"Tour the countryside? There are still a lot of areas out there that don't even have electricity, you know."

She finished her drink in one gulp, then placed it firmly on the coffee table before her. "Let's go to bed," she said, looking at the empty glass.

That took him by surprise. Kira had been distant

ever since they'd left the Center. She was too quiet—he wasn't used to these moods and attitudes. And now, all of a sudden, she wanted to have sex. It didn't make sense. She seemed distrustful and depressed.

"Why? Just to get it over with?" he asked.

She looked at him slowly, deliberately, until her eyes penetrated the defenses he'd erected and grabbed his heart, twisting it, hurting it. "Yes. Just to get it over with."

Dennis tossed off the mescanol and got up to get another. As he walked, the floor beneath his feet shifted, changed, became something totally different. It took him a moment to realize that it was the mescanol taking effect. He poured himself another four fingers and downed it quickly. It was smooth. When he turned and looked around, it was a different room.

He found his way through the mescanol mist: the shimmering crushed-jewel floor made of opals, emeralds, and turquoise, sparkling and dancing in the fluid light; the melting plastic furniture dissolving and collecting in pools; the insane colors bursting and forming into patterns on the walls, and kissed her.

It was so much easier with the mescanol.

She pushed him away. "Wait, Dennis. Wait a minute." He moved back. "I can't do it like this. I thought I could, but I can't. It's no good."

Her lips tasted leathery—dry and rough, and when he'd slipped his arms around her, she'd felt warm. Very warm.

"What . . . what . . . do you mean?" he asked.

She got up from the couch and went to the bar. He watched her pass through phantoms and ethereal shapes as she poured herself a drink. "Want one?" she asked.

He nodded. "Mescanol?"

"Sure. Why not."

She poured his drink and started walking back toward him. She took two steps, then burst into flames. He heard her flesh sizzle and the flames crackle as the top layer of her skin burned away. The smell reached him and he started to gag. He smothered a scream and leapt to his feet, took a jerky, hesitant step forward, then froze.

The mescanol. It was the mescanol. That's all it is, he thought. The mescanol. It's over. It's over.

"Here," Kira said, offering him his drink, smiling.

Eyes wide, heart pounding, he watched her blazing body come closer, hands outstretched. Flesh from her fingers drifted to the floor like crisps of burned paper.

"Here," she repeated.

He looked away and accepted the glass; it was cool to the touch. It couldn't continue that much longer—the hallucination was no more than that: a hallucination. It's over. It's over. Too much mescanol. He shook his head savagely, trying to clear it of the horrifying images.

"Is something wrong?" she asked.

"Wrong? No, I ... I'm, uhm ... forget it." He sat across from her and sipped his drink. Her blackened legs were crossed at the ankles.

"It's no good, Dennis. We're not the same people anymore."

"What ... what do you ... mean?" he managed to ask, trying to look at anything but the liquid fire that crept from her eyes and flowed down her cheeks to leave fiery, burning trails.

She shook her head, leaned forward, and set her glass on the table. "I don't think it can work out. It's over."

It's over, it's over, he echoed in his mind.

"You think I did it, don't you?" he said from between clenched teeth.

"No, it's not that."

He got up. He couldn't watch her anymore. He couldn't stand it. He was losing control. A few deep breaths. Turn and pace. Watch the distracting pretty colors on the wall. Leap off the balcony. Anything, but don't look at her.

"What is it, then? I don't understand, Kira," he said, back to her trying to ignore the crackling sound in his ears.

"It's . . . well, it's what you do."

He turned around and looked at her, not thinking of what he might have to see. "What do I do that's so bad?" he asked, nearly shouting. She looked normal.

"Your job. The slime you go to parties with, shake hands with, kiss and grab. I can't stand them. And I can't stand *you* since you've started to like it."

Her eyes were cold and hard, her anger so real he could almost feel waves of it reaching him.

"I'll quit," he said.

"Sure. You always quit. How many times did you quit last week?" She realized what she'd said, her time sense still disoriented, and shook her head. "Oh, no, sorry. Well, you know what I mean."

"I know. And I understand."

"You do?"

"Yes." He put his drink down beside her empty glass and sat down. "I do. You forget—we've been through this before. You don't remember it, and I understand that, but I meant what I said. I will quit."

"You mean it this time? 'Cause Dennis, this is it. I can't stay with you any longer if you still want to be a procurer. I mean it. I couldn't take it."

"I mean it," he said.

She shook her head. "No matter how much I love you, or you love me, if living together is going to make me depressed most of the time, then I'd just as soon have the marriage nullified."

"Baby, you mean more to me than that job, or any job. I only got into it for you, so we'd have money for . . . for . . . whatever we needed. That's all. I don't like rubbing elbows with those people. And I'd like it less now."

"Then you really would quit?" she asked, hope in her sparkling eyes, her soft voice, her tense, coiled muscles.

He nodded.

She threw her arms around him and kissed his cheek, his neck, and when he managed to turn his head, his lips. She was giggling and crying at the same time.

But there was something different about her. She felt different. Somehow, her skin was rougher, her perfume offensive rather than alluring. And all he could think about was what he wanted to do to Freddie, Mara, Oleo, and Howard.

"What do you think you'd like to do instead?" she asked, still excited.

"Huh?"

"Plans, you know? Future job opportunities? Or would you like me to work for awhile?"

"Oh. I hadn't really thought about it. There's time."

She sighed happily. "Yes, I guess there is."

Tell her. She would have to find out sooner or later. Tell her now. Don't do this to her. She deserves to know. Tell her. She would probably agree with what you've got planned for them since they murdered her. Killed. Dead. Reconstructed. Changed. "Listen, Kira, I *am* going to quit, but—"

"But? What's that supposed to mean? I thought. . . ."

She stiffened at his side, and he knew it was useless to try and explain to her what had to be done. He couldn't tell her. And there was another reason why he had to go back: he couldn't just abandon his clients and angels, no matter what kind of people they were. And they were people he still felt responsibility toward. Never going back at least to make sure

Mary's reconstruction came off properly would have been unthinkable.

"I can't just quit. A few of my clients already have angels. They're waiting for me to work out the details for them."

"One of your . . . associates could do that. You don't have to go back."

He shook his head. "No. There's no one I could trust to handle things properly. I can't afford to trust them."

"Can't you just let those people fend for themselves? What do you care about them for?" she asked, hoping that she might somehow convince him.

He shook his head again. "Sorry, baby. I've got to finish what I've started. That's the way I am. I can't just leave them there, waiting. It'll probably be a few days. It shouldn't take that long." Unless, he thought, the Franks, Johnson and Warren decide to leave the city at the same time and make it impossible for me to get them all.

"A few days, huh?"

He nodded.

She moved away from him. "I don't believe you. There's something else to this. You can't quit. You couldn't quit even if you wanted to. You love the business too much."

He raised his hand, anger coursing through him like a flash flood, but managed to stop himself before hitting her. He saw the fear in her eyes, the conclusion she had reached, as he lowered his hand to his lap.

"The marriage is off," she said with a finality that hurt.

"You say you love me, Kira? Well, I'm going to give you the chance to prove it."

"I'm not interested in proving anything. I know what I feel—I don't have to prove it to you."

"That's not what I mean. All I'm asking is that you give me a chance. That's all—just a chance. Let me go back home and straighten things out, settle my business affairs. I can't just walk out like I was never in the business. There are people waiting for me, depending on me for new lives, new chances, and I don't like the idea of letting them down. Give me the time I need to get everything in order. Give me that time before you make up your mind."

She looked at her empty glass. She picked his up and took a swallow of mescanol. Dennis waited. She took another swallow, then put the glass down. There was so much more he wanted to explain but he stopped himself. He didn't want to stay with her if he had to talk her into anything—what kind of relationship would that be? She would have to show him she loved and trusted him enough to let him prove his sincerity and his love for her.

"You want it all your way, don't you?" she asked.

He was about to explain and defend himself but she waved him off.

"All right. You've got your chance. When we were in the Center I agreed to a ten day trial. We've got nine days left. If you quit before the ten days are up, we'll have something to talk about."

He smiled, his emotions bursting out from the prison deep inside, and reached for her. She backed away.

"Nine days," she said coldly.

And he knew then that she meant it.

It was possible to settle things in nine days, but in order to do so he would have to leave tonight. He'd have to go straight to Bentwell's and find them. Yes, he thought, it was possible.

And he looked forward to seeing Freddie Frank in a way he'd never before felt.

Good old Freddie Frank.

24

Right above the doorway leading into one of Bentwell's smaller lounges was a sign: *Freddie's Place.* Small tables and smaller chairs were scattered around the room like mushrooms; a bar, complete with bartender supplied by Bentwell, lined the entire far wall; maces, shields, swords, sabers, daggers, and carbines, as well as holos of electric chairs, gas chambers, and concentration camps were tastefully placed, hanging from the ceiling and mounted on the walls to give the lounge that homey feeling that Freddie Frank liked.

He was proud of that place. Couples, threesomes, and small groups of people some with "BI" patches sewn on their chests, sat around, talked and joked, made promises to each other they had no intention of keeping, smiling with their mouths and perpetual caresses; but not with their eyes. And they were all Freddie's friends. Freddie's guests. Freddie's angels. After all, they deserved to be comfortable. They deserved the best.

Mara sat across from him. Her sweater had distracting cut-outs that revealed her bare breasts and rouged nipples; the material of her bolero pants could have been sprayed on from an aerosol can. He had to admire the way she looked, and the way she worked. She had developed a cheshire cat smile, and was using it, along with the rest of her body, to her best advantage. She was listening to one of the many, letting the point of her tongue slide back and forth across her glistening lips, soaking up everything he said, nodding in all the right places, helping Freddie harvest the never-ending line of prospects, weeding out the elite from the riffraff. It was a new experience for the both of them; they had never before had the opportunity to pick and choose.

Freddie knew Mara was good at it—as good as Dennis had ever been. He was glad he'd decided to wait before killing her; she handled the prospects deftly, manipulating and playing with them as if they were toys. Still, there was always that chance with Mara—she could wake up any afternoon and decide that Freddie was no more than an albatross, and that her neck was getting tired with him hanging there. He kept a watchful eye on her, never really trusting, never letting his guard down.

"I'm going to walk around a little," he told her.

She smiled and nodded; he was dismissed.

He got up and stretched, luxuriating in the feeling. He felt better than he had in years, and he had Dennis Lange to thank for it. Or Lange's angels, he thought.

Freddie drank only the best booze, aged in real wood casks, ate only the finest, choicest cuts of meat, the freshest vegetables, smoked only the best of the best dope, and got invitations to all the openings around town, and even to some on the other coast. He was finally someone. Someone important.

He was on top.

He glanced around the crowded little lounge, then decided to make his rounds and say hello to some of his friends. It had taken Bentwell two weeks to realize what was good for him, Freddie thought as he walked. And he still doesn't accept the fact that I'm here to stay. Why the hell does he insist on fighting me? He knows I'm his only hope. He knows I'm going to take over sooner or later. If I stopped coming to this place he'd be out of business so fast he wouldn't even know what hit him.

I ought to leave and let this crummy place fold. Yeah. It would serve him right—teach the dumb bastard a lesson. Show him who's the boss.

He knew that Bentwell was a chump, a patsy easily manipulated. The night after Freddie had taken care of Dennis, he'd lied a little, anticipating Dennis's reaction. He'd told Bentwell that Dennis had quit the business, that he and Kira were having terrible marital problems, and that Dennis had asked him to take over all of his clients and angels. Bentwell had found that difficult to believe at first, but when Dennis never came in, and after Freddie had embellished his story, Bentwell had no other choice but to give in to Freddie's demands. No other procurers would be allowed inside the small lounge, and Bentwell's fee would be adjusted in Freddie's favor. Dennis's clients and angels came over slowly, but by the time Freddie had finished redecorating the lounge, they were all his.

For Bentwell, it was a question of business, and who could do the most for his credit balance. Freddie had been quick and smart enough to point this out. Without the procurer's fees, Bentwell couldn't—

"Hey, Mr. Frank!" a woman at a table said as he passed. Rather nice on the eyes.

"Hi."

—stay open, and with everyone waiting for Dennis to get back, there were no fees.

He had taken care of Dennis, all right. No one in Bentwell's even remembered the bastard. Once a procurer was gone, he was gone for good.

And good old Henri had helped. He shook his head, amazed at what Mara's ex-husband had accomplished. It hadn't been hard to find someone willing and able to forge the necessary signatures on the forms the Center required, but without that dinner with Henri the signatures would never have been authenticated and verified. Henri's high position in the Administration Complex had made the plan work.

And it had worked perfectly.

He swung his riding crop as he walked and, with each stride, he pointed it at someone, giving them a smile or a wink. Keep the customers smiling and satisfied.

Lange had to be scared off; the idiot was probably too busy explaining things to his wife to do anything about it. He must have seen that Freddie meant business, that he was playing for keeps. He must have gone into another line of work—something less risky, something less profitable. Lange had always been afraid for his own skin.

He glanced at the doorway. Two couples were strolling through the entrance. He couldn't make out the face on the second man though—it was partially blocked by the other man, but he was about the right height and did have black hair. Everything stopped for Freddie in that moment, as he devoted his full concentration to the man. He froze, ready to draw his needle gun.

Then the first man moved and Freddie saw the second man's face. He resumed breathing.

"Hi, Freddie," a young man said. His voice was eager, excited.

Freddie smiled, the layer of skin beneath the baby-face makeup cracking, making him think the makeup might be cracking, too. "Hi. I haven't seen you around here before, have I?"

The young man shook his head and half-rose from his chair, extending his hand. "Andy Legget," he said.

Freddie shook the young man's hand and sat in an empty chair, facing the doorway. "Mind if I sit?"

"No, not at all."

"Your first time here?"

"Oh, no. I've been to Bentwell's, but I never visited your lounge before. This is some setup you got here."

"Well, thanks. I'm glad you like it."

"I should say so. I spent quite a few evenings wandering around out there looking for a decent procurer but they're all second-rate slobs."

"I see," Freddie said, not seeing at all. He hadn't the slightest idea what, if anything, Legget was getting at. He wished Mara had come along—she could have been sitting beside him right now, listening to what this young punk was saying. She would have known how to respond, how to phrase the response properly, how to find out what Legget wanted without making her confusion obvious.

"You know, it's really a pleasure to watch someone like you work," Legget said.

Now what was that supposed to mean? "Why, thanks," Freddie said. "Most people take what I do for granted. Either that or they just don't like to think about it."

Legget bobbed his head in agreement. "Yeah. I know what you mean."

A pitch. Here comes the pitch, Freddie realized. I should have seen it coming—I should have expected it. Damn. "Oh, do you really?"

Legget nodded again. "Yeah. Lemme tell you, I seen all kinds of procurers, but I never seen anyone work like you do. Why, just the number of people you grind through in an evening is amazing all by itself."

Freddie smiled. That was true enough. This Legget was pretty perceptive for such a young guy. He was right. It was a pleasure to talk to someone who knew what was going on, someone who could appreciate the finer talents that Freddie had to employ. "Well, thanks. Thanks a lot."

"Sure. Don't mention it."

Where was the pitch? Maybe there wasn't any. Yeah. That would be fine. Maybe the kid was just awed by the skill and charm he exuded through his pores. The smile on his face grew, pumping up his pride, inflating his ego, swelling, almost bursting and gushing over like an orgasm. He stood and motioned toward the bar with his hand.

"Care to join me in a friendly drink?" Freddie offered.

Legget's eyes lit as if they were powered by a laser. "Yeah. I sure would."

He followed Freddie across the room to the bar.

They sat on comfortable stools, facing the mirror that covered the wall behind the bar. Freddie watched the movements and patterns the people made in the mirror as they drifted from one table to another, trying to make something happen that only Freddie could. He glanced at the doorway's reflection.

"Yes, sir, Mr. Frank?" the bartender said, standing before them.

"Were you fixing a drink?" Freddie asked.

"Well, I was, sort of."

He slammed his riding crop to the bar; it cracked like a whip. "What do you mean, sort of? Either you were or you weren't."

"I was, sir."

"Then go back there and finish. And when you're done, I'll order. Not until."

"Yes, sir."

The bartender smiled meekly and went back to preparing the drink. Freddie knew he could afford to be gracious now. It was no longer a case of waiting for the bartender to get around to him—he was the host, putting the needs of his guests above his own.

"Not every procurer would have done that," Legget observed.

Freddie shrugged. "Any good one would've. It's important that your angels are satisfied." He poked

Legget in the ribs with an elbow. "And I don't mean just sexually, either."

Legget let out a high-pitched laugh.

"What are *you* interested in?"

Legget shrugged. "I don't know."

"Sexually, I mean. You can tell me. Anything special?"

"Oh, I see. No, nothing out of the ordinary, I suppose. I guess I might have given you the wrong impression. You see, I'm not interested in using your services. I'm more interested in learning from you. A man with your skill at handling people would be the perfect person for me to learn from."

"Learn? To be a procurer?"

"Yeah. If you let me hang around, I could learn. I could even help out with some . . . things."

Freddie smiled patronizingly. "Really, now? And what could you do for me?"

"I could talk to Bentwell."

"About what?" Freddie asked.

"About that second lounge you need."

"What second lounge?"

Legget shook his head in obvious admiration. "You're good, Freddie. One of the very best. Now I know how you got to be so big."

What the hell was that supposed to mean? What was he talking about? Freddie wondered. He glanced quickly at the doorway's reflection in the mirror. "Well, I try."

Legget chuckled. "I should say so. Do you want me to talk to him for you? I can be very persuasive."

So I see, Freddie thought. A second lounge, huh? Not a bad idea. That would be fine. Just fine. And there wouldn't be any reason to stop there, either. With Bentwell weakened, a second lounge would probably cement Freddie's position.

"Let's talk money first. You seem to be capable —I'd hate to underpay you and lose you later on." He dropped his baby-faced smile and facade and stared at him until he was sure the boy was uncomfortable. "If you know what I mean."

"I understand."

"Good."

Freddie was pleased. They discussed business and settled on a salary, and then he told Legget to talk to Bentwell, but to be nice and very polite. He explained that this would be a warm-up, and that he wasn't to pressure Bentwell at all.

Before Legget got up to leave, Freddie grabbed his forearm. "You're raw, kid. You really haven't got the slightest idea how I got to the top. Don't make me show you. If you do, you'll regret it."

"Don't worry about me," Legget said nervously, finally realizing the situation he'd gotten himself into. "I'm not looking to take over anything—I'm just looking to earn a little money while I learn some things."

Freddie released his arm. "Yeah, fine. Now get lost."

"Sure."

He carefully watched Legget's reflection as he walked out of the lounge, not really sure why, but definitely looking for something. He continued to stare long after the kid was gone, tensing up as each man with dark hair and average height came through the doorway. When one man entered, accompanied by a woman with short blonde hair, Freddie's hand leaped for his needle gun.

He knew what he was looking for. He prayed Mara was right.

He prayed he never found him.

25

The empty airport terminal reminded Dennis of a stadium an hour after the big game had ended. A few porters and cab drivers wandered around, smoked, talked to each other, looking for ways to make the night pass quickly, while businessmen in their suits stood like rusted iron statues, waiting for the tinny nasal voice to announce the boarding of the flight. It was the last flight out of Mexico City; the last incoming flight had debarked an hour earlier.

When the plane finally took off, Dennis was relieved to find that he had most of the plane to himself. He wouldn't be bothered by the inane ramblings of the too-fat tourists, or by the oily businessmen who needed someone to talk to, to pour out their loneliness to—someone willing to listen to the emptiness of their success.

The plane droned on through the night blackness, soothing him, lulling him, relaxing him enough so that thinking was no longer a painful experience.

He knew what he wanted to do, what he had to do.

He didn't think that things with Kira would ever

really be the same. Not any more. Too much had happened this time; some of the events had far-lasting effects. It hurt to think about it, to remember what their one day had been like in that miserable hotel suite. It hurt to remember that the reconciliation that had once taken place had been for nothing; neither one of them had thought to update their crystals then.

And what was there to updating a crystal? It was totally safe, painless, and took less than a minute. That's all it would have taken, Dennis thought. Just sit in the special chair and let the beams do their work. All they did was scan your brain from two different angles of entry. Where they met, they analyzed.

Less than a minute.

While the beams scanned your brain, two other beams scanned the crystal and produced an analogous representation of the flesh and blood point. The beams scanned so quickly, they covered every synapse, every neuron, every fiber and cell in the brain in less than a minute. When it was done, the crystal held a still-life image, a frozen duplicate of the brain, right down to the smallest thought, the weakest memory.

It's going to take me longer than that to kill Freddie Frank, he thought. It's going to take him longer than that to die. And it's not going to be painless.

Not for him.

No. Not for him.

"Did you say something, sir?" a stewardess asked. It stood in the aisle, unmoving, unthinking, capable of nothing other than what its microprocessor had been programed for.

"No, no thanks," Dennis said.

The stewardess rolled down the aisle.

Dennis realized he was going to have to be careful. He couldn't just walk into Bentwell's and kill Freddie. And he knew himself well enough to realize that if he didn't think, didn't plan, he would do just that.

He closed his eyes and savored an image, a fantasy in which his hands were firmly clasped around Freddie's fat throat, his thumbs pressing tighter and tighter into Freddie's windpipe. Fear and blind panic lit Freddie's dull eyes and saliva dribbled down his chin; his tongue stretched out like a writhing snake; his arms and hands thrashed about madly, wildly, searching in vain for something to grab, something to defend himself with.

Dennis chuckled.

"Did you say something, sir?" a stewardess asked from the aisle. "Can I be of some help?"

"Yes, sure. Self destruct."

"I am sorry, sir, but that operation is not listed anywhere among my instruction programs. If you—"

"Leave me alone," Dennis said. "Forget it."

The stewardess rolled on down the aisle.

Pain in the ass, Dennis thought. I would have been better off with a planeload of tourists, or even a bridge club.

He closed his eyes and tried to recapture the fantasy, but it had gone.

Well, that was all right. Strangulation took a long time, and in that way it did fit the requirements, but it lacked subtlety. Dennis knew he could do better than that. It would also be tiring and require absolute privacy, a situation he was not likely to come across with Freddie. No, he realized, strangulation would not do at all.

He smiled.

There was a book. A present from one of his steadier angels. It held a lot of interesting information —some of it was obscure, some of it was too detailed and drawn out, but it was still his best bet. It was home, tucked away in some dusty corner, almost buried on a shelf in his den. Maybe one of its pages would hold the answer to Freddie Frank's fate.

But what a shame, he thought, wasting Freddie by the book. Dennis had always been original, thinking up new scenes and variations on old ones for his angels, and it was something Dennis was proud of. It was the least he could do for himself.

And for Freddie.

After all, he *was* quitting the business.

26

Dennis opened the front door of his house. It was dark, quiet, and deserted inside, and he was in no rush to enter. The book would be helpful if he used it properly, and he knew this, but crossing the threshold and walking into the house was not an easy thing for him. Kira was still in Mexico City waiting for his return. The house had been shut down for ten days; it no longer seemed like his home—it was only a structure: a house.

He shrugged off his anxiety and forged into the hallway. Once inside the house he felt a little better, a little safer. He felt along the left wall, looking for the control panel. It sprang open with a light pressure from his finger, and he located the main switch.

As he touched it, the lights clicked on. The air conditioning came to life, relays clicked, servos hummed, the microprocessors took stock of the house's state and made the necessary adjustments; he was home.

He retrieved his bags from the porch and set them down by the front door. There was time for unpacking later—if he stayed in the city that long. If things went well, he might not even have to unpack.

He made straight for the den.

He rummaged around the shelves until he found the book. It was old, its binding cracked, its pages brown and brittle with age. He handled it carefully.

METHODS AND TECHNIQUES: AN AID IN SELECTION

CONTENTS

Dennis closed the book carefully. He wasn't sure he liked what he'd seen. Granted, if used properly, the book could be a tremendous aid, but this matter was personal, and he wasn't pleased with his need for an outside stimulus.

Nonetheless, a little research never hurt, he thought.

He rechecked the table of contents and opened the book to page 157.

HALLUCINOGENS
USES: TOXIC PSYCHOSIS & DISORIENTATION

ALKALOIDS
*ATROPINE
AYAHUASCA (YAGE)
BANISTERIOPSIS
BELLADONNA
CANNABIS
DATURA
DET
DMT
HENBANE (HYOSCYAMUS)
*HYOSCYAMINE
KAWA
LSD
MANDRAGORA (MANDRAKE)
MESCALINE
MESCANOL
MUSHROOMS
PEYOTE
PSILOCYBIN
*SCOPOLAMINE

Those chemicals starred (*) are recommended for specific uses in cases where the victim is distrustful or suspects the potential use of hallucinogens.

These starred chemicals are parasympatholytic agents, producing toxic psychosis characterized by a high degree of excitement, intensely uncomfortable side effects, and amnesia for the experience.

Atropine and scopolamine (though less so for hyoscyamine) are both recommended hallucinogens as they can be absorbed through unbroken skin. LSD, when highly concentrated and in liquid form, is also useful in this same manner. Atropine and scopolamine are powerful drugs whose effects can easily be mistaken for ordinary toxic psychosis.

There was no need for Dennis to read further in that section of the book. He had gotten what little information he felt he might need. He flipped back to the table of contents, ignoring the loud cracking sound the binding made as it split down the middle. He turned to page 298.

ACIDS

HYDROCHLORIC ACID (HCl): Excellent for throwing. Sharp odor, due to its toxic fumes. If a sufficient quantity of these fumes is inhaled, choking and shutdown of the respiratory tract can occur. A more salient application of this acid, though, is in contact with skin. It can burn its way through flesh. . . .

NITRIC ACID (HNO$_3$): Will eat skin. . . .

SULFURIC ACID (H$_2$SO$_4$ · H$_2$O): Will eat skin, but it is a far superior overall acid to either *nitric* or *hydrochloric*. When mixed with water,

large amounts of heat are released. If mixed slowly, while being constantly stirred, no damage may
be done. But when mixed haphazardly violent
vaporization may result, splattering the solution
on the face, hands, or other exposed portions of
the body. . . .

That was enough for the acids, Dennis thought.
They were a messy way to deal with somebody. But
then, Freddie didn't deserve a clean, quick death. He
let the book rest in his lap and leaned back, relaxing
for a few moments.

He slipped off his shoes and rubbed his tired feet.
He needed a drink. But first, there was something else
he wanted to check. He thumbed back to the contents
page and found what he was looking for. It was a
fairly large section, and it started on page 83.

POISONS

POISONOUS PLANTS: MUSHROOMS

AMANITA: A very poisonous mushroom
that can easily be mistaken for a safe, non-toxic
mushroom. One of the genus Amanita, the
Amanita phalloides (the death cap), looks like
an edible mushroom and tastes very good. . . .

Dennis skimmed the rest of the mushrooms and
stopped to read the section's summation.

In general, all mushrooms with white gills
have an extremely good likelihood of being toxic.
These can create severe abdominal pain three to
six hours after ingestion. Diarrhea, vomiting, and

jaundice follow. Death comes from failure of the liver. Sweating and delirious reactions, as well as hallucinations, may occur with some varieties of mushrooms.

(SEE ALSO HALLUCINOGENS: P. 157)

He closed the book and put it back on the shelf. There was really little there he could use, except possibly the information on atropine and sulfuric acid. That interested him. It went along nicely with something he'd managed to work out on the plane—something that was fitting, that held a certain amount of charm, risk, and retribution.

He decided to change clothes and take the time to think it over. His bare feet sank into the yielding floor as he walked to the hallway to retrieve his suitcase.

He missed Kira. He was sorry she wasn't there to see and participate in what would happen. But it wasn't worth the risk of having her with him—things might not go as planned.

He had already decided to save Freddie for last.

27

It was mid-morning; sunlight poured through the bedroom window in golden shafts, danced off airborne dust particles that sparkled like a billion tiny gems. Dennis stretched luxuriously and relaxed, the tension in his body gone after the deep though short sleep. He sat up in bed, and the suspensor field adjusted to the new distribution of weight.

He braced himself unconsciously for the second shift in the field that normally followed like a wave, but it didn't come. Kira wasn't there to roll over in her sleep as she usually did when he sat up.

Sleeping without her had been difficult, especially in their own bed. It had been hard enough while he was at the Center, but that had been different. She belonged here—she was in every corner, every centimeter of the room. His mind and body were geared to expect certain movements while he slept beside her, certain noises, too, and none of them had been there. He felt alone—more alone than ever before.

He was afraid she wouldn't try again. There was no reason why she should believe him this time—he had broken that same promise before. And even if she did agree to try, nothing would be certain. Not ever again.

Freddie had fixed that. Freddie and Mara and Oleo and Howard. Dennis took great pleasure in hating them for that.

He had reasons enough for what he was going to do. He even had the old worn book to help him if he needed it. He got up, went to the bathroom, then dressed.

It was going to be a good day.

As he watched the breakfast menu flash by on the screen in the kitchen, he hummed a bouncy, happy tune he'd heard in the airport terminal the night before. He selected a healthy breakfast and settled into the breakfast nook to eat.

He thought about the first order of business for the day as he finished off the fried kippers. Howard Warren. The jealous, indignant neophyte. The tyro. One of the slimy butchers. One of the mercenaries.

He took a sip of coffee, then smeared a spoonful of black raspberry jam on the last slice of toast.

There were ways to kill, and then there were ways to kill, he thought. And Howard Warren could be dealt with most easily, most simply, without having to leave the house.

He finished eating, then crossed the kitchen to place his dirty dishes into the washer. He returned to the nook and started to dial the phone number, then stopped. He hit the disconnect button. He took a few deep breaths, then got up and casually walked into the living room.

Warren would be the first one to go. It was a delicious and delicate moment—he wanted to prolong the excitement, revel in it, surround himself in it as if it were a warm, snug, safe womb. He wanted to live there, not come out, mete out his justice with an invisible but powerful hand. And once that phone number had been dialed, there would be no turning back, no time for second thoughts. He would have to follow it through to the end.

There was no need to rush headlong into it. He would take his time and think it through once more, make sure he really wanted these people dead. He selected a small throw pillow from the couch and strolled back into the kitchen with it.

This time he was sure.

He placed the pillow on the nook's hard wooden bench, sat on it in front of the phone screen, then entered the number.

His stomach lurched for an instant as the connection clicked and the phone rang; he smoothed back his black hair and licked his lips.

"Administration Complex," a young, good-looking man said.

Dennis beamed one of his better smiles. "Good morning. Chief Supervisor Warren, please."

The man smiled back. "One moment." He turned to his left to face the data terminal, pressed a few keys, waited a moment, then turned back to Dennis. His smile was replaced by a look of confusion. "I'm sorry, sir, but there is no chief supervisor named Warren working here."

Dennis shook his head, still smiling. "I'm sure there is. You must be mistaken. That can't be right." He hoped he wasn't putting it on too much. "He told me he was a chief supervisor. Would you check it again, please? Perhaps he's not a chief."

The man smiled again, then nodded. "Yes, certainly, sir. One moment." He turned to the screen on his left and consulted the list of supervisors. "I'm sorry, but there are no supervisors by that name, either. Could you tell me the full name?"

"Certainly. Howard Warren."

The receptionist pressed more keys to his left, waited a long moment, then turned back to Dennis, still looking confused. "I'm sorry, sir, but the only Howard Warren I show is employed as a clerk."

"A clerk?"

"Yes, sir."

"You're positive?"

"Yes, sir," the man said, nodding. "Perhaps you're mistaken about the name?"

"No, I am not," Dennis said, letting anger and outrage enter his tone. "And you people won't hear the end of this, I promise you! The police will hear about this."

"Yes, sir," the man said, blanching. "We would appreciate it if you would hold for a moment. I'd like you to speak to Mr. Warren's departmental chief."

Good, Dennis thought. Standard procedure when someone starts to complain about someone else. Pass the buck. It was going to work—he could feel it. "I'll hold," he said as if having trouble controlling his anger.

Before the young man's image faded from the screen, Dennis saw relief clearly written on his face. The screen went black as the extension rang. A click, then another man's face filled the screen.

"Cooper, here," the man said. He wore antique wire-frame glasses. Hiding behind the lenses were quick brown eyes. He had a thin face and a thin, hawk-like nose. He seemed hyperkinetic, as if the least likely place for him was behind a desk.

"Hello, Mr. Cooper. The receptionist put me through to you."

Cooper nodded, motioned with his hand for Dennis to start talking. Dennis didn't like the man's attitude.

"I'll call back some other time—after I've had a chance to talk to my attorney, when you're not quite so busy," Dennis said, reaching forward for the disconnect switch.

"No, wait!" Cooper said. "I'm sorry. I was in the middle of something. I didn't mean to see uninterested."

"I understand."

"I take it you have some sort of problem?"

Dennis nodded.

"Why don't you tell me what happened?"

"Well, it's rather difficult for me to explain—I'm not quite sure what this whole thing means or how many people in your organization are involved. But before I say anything specific, I want your word that you'll keep my name out of this. I can't afford a scandal. Luckily, no harm was done; but harm was meant."

"I don't quite understand," Cooper said.

"All right. You see, my name is Bruce Kelly. I'm the head of the Confederation of Scouts. . . ."

"Yes?"

"I was contacted by one of your staff, a Mr. Howard Warren, and was offered some very specific and peculiar services. He presented himself as a chief supervisor, and said this was a new policy of the Administration Complex. . . ."

"And just what did he offer you, Mr. Kelly?"

"Access to private records and files."

Cooper's face underwent a transformation. His lips stretched tightly over a row of perfect white teeth, exposing a set of sharp canines, and his forehead wrinkled in concern. "I see. I'm glad you told me about this. You say he presented himself as a chief supervisor?"

Dennis nodded. "Yes. I was calling to explain to him that my organization is not geared toward the more nefarious schemes he seemed to be so taken with. Well, when I asked for his office, the receptionist checked and told me that he was a clerk, and not a chief supervisor. He isn't even a supervisor!"

Cooper looked down at his desk and shuffled papers aside until he found a row of keys and buttons that connected to the data terminal mounted on the edge of his desk. He pressed several buttons, waited a moment, then looked back at Dennis.

"Here it is, Mr. Kelly. The receptionist was right. Howard Warren is employed as a clerk."

"You mean he *was* a clerk, don't you?" Dennis asked.

Cooper nodded. "Thank you for the correction. I did mean was."

Dennis sat back in his chair, arms behind his head, smiling. He knew what Cooper was doing, how strict and tight internal security was within the Complex. Warren was probably in one of the interrogation rooms right now, fidgeting, fighting for his job, denying everything, trying to figure out what was happening and who the hell Kelly was.

But Dennis knew it would do him no good.

The Complex's security would easily dig up every particle of information, every piece of Warren's past, and Dennis knew what they would find, and what conclusion they would jump to.

And Howard Warren would do the rest, all by himself.

28

When they finally let Howard Warren go, he was a dead man. Security had barely scratched the surface of his past when they found he had established credit at Bentwell's. With a little more pawing through the computer's records, they found he had participated in an expensive evening with Albert Johnson, the broker, at the Center. A quick but thorough check of his salary, expenses, and credit balance proved to be sufficient evidence for immdiate action.

Warren calmly settled himself in behind the controls of the car and stared blindly through the windshield into space. He sat motionless, barely breathing, as the sky slowly dimmed and the clouds took on the melting colors of the sunset. Dusk settled, and a lone point of light, the first star, appeared high over the clear top of the car. A flying insect landed on the outside of the glass and walked around, testing, tasting, and flew off. The car made a soft creaking and pinging sound as the metal body cooled in the coming evening.

When the lights in the parking lot sprang to life, flooding the area with magnesium brilliance, Warren blinked, then bent his right leg, lifting his foot up and even with the car's control console. He closed his eyes and clamped his teeth together till his jaw ached, then kicked forward, straightening his leg with all his might.

He hadn't done it out of anger.

What kind of anger could a dead man feel?

A one-timer. If he was lucky, another fifty years or so before worm food.

He had to drive using the manual controls. He'd ruined the automatic guidance system.

Paula would probably be home from her job, involved in some holoshow or book, letting the kitchen cook supper, worried about why he was so late getting home.

The apartment was small, cluttered, messy; a crumbling group of rooms in a low-income building. Warren knew they could afford to move and live better, get a bigger place in a nicer area, but he also realized what that would have meant. Crystals were expensive.

He had lost his job. And in doing so, had lost a lot more than just a place to spend his days. There was no longer the chance of paying for his crystal and reconstruction. He was a dead man just as surely as if someone had walked up to him, pointed an antique revolver to his head, and pulled the trigger.

Warren even knew who had loaded the gun.

The neighborhood was dirty: crumbling curbs; cracked and littered sidewalks; walls of buildings covered with graffiti; people whose faces were made of leather, whose skin sagged at their cheeks like squirrels storing nuts; all surrounded and enveloped in the foul stench of decay. He was home. He parked the car in the ground-level garage, then took the elevator down to the floor his apartment was on.

The hallways were crowded, as usual: children played noisily, all too aware of the future they would soon have to face; men and women sat on the floor, their hollow eyes always searching for a way to get the money they needed; dust addicts who had stolen, lied, or killed their way into enough money to pay for their crystals prepared themselves for their painful reconstruction at the hands of an angel.

Warren didn't want to end up like them.

He was happier being a dead man.

He unlocked the door to his apartment and entered, double locking it behind himself out of habit.

"Hi, Paula. I'm home," he said.

He heard the mental hello but felt the empty pit deep inside when his ears heard nothing but his own breathing. It was the same thing every day since she'd left, almost a month ago.

"What's for dinner?" he asked, going directly into the bedroom. He rummaged through the left half of the dresser, *his* side, searching for the needles. He knew where the gun was, but the blue needles ... he couldn't remember where he'd put them.

The yellow ones were good, but they wouldn't kill.

He opened the empty drawers on Paula's side; they slid open easily, weightlessly, as if they were made of paper.

"That's fine, dear," he shouted in the direction of the kitchen.

Now, where the hell were those needles? To hell with them, he decided. The yellow ones would have to do. He was already dead; maybe he wouldn't need the blue ones.

He changed his clothes, brushed his wavy hair straight back, trimmed his mustache, said good-bye to Paula, then went out.

Warren didn't want to take the chance of missing him; he got there early, before all of Bentwell's came alive. He sat in Freddie's Place sipping a gin and tonic, coolly thinking about the best course of action once Freddie walked through the doorway. So far, only two other people were in the lounge, and they were both at the bar, to Warren's left. One was the bartender, getting ready for the evening; the other was a young, volatile-looking man.

Warren waited patiently.

People drifted in slowly. At first it was just couples seeking some privacy in the almost-empty lounge, sitting at the corner booths and tables. The young man at the bar nodded to everyone, gave them each a toothy smile. Warren figured he was probably a regular, waiting for some young and attractive man or woman to come in.

A group of five entered and approached the bar. One of the men called the young man by name and treated him with what Warren felt was too much respect for his age. The man had called him Legget. The name and face meant nothing to Warren.

No one approached to offer Warren a drink or to sit down and talk. His clothes, his hair, his very mannerisms separated him from the others like a wall, making him feel like a pariah. He drank slowly but steadily, using up what little credit he had.

He started to get bored and thought of getting up and walking around to see how the big crowd in the main lounge was shaping up. Bentwell's had once been a dream, a fairyland where real people played and lived, a place he could never have entered without the help of his cousin's membership card. But the place had lost its mystery—he knew what he was to these people. Since he had done that favor for Freddie he had a permanent invitation, and had used it twice. Twice had been enough. He missed Paula. He continued to sit, uncomfortable at the small mushroom-shaped table, sipping his drink, very bored, waiting for Freddie's arrival, letting the slick people amuse themselves with something other than himself.

The young man at the bar, Legget, was staring at him. His bar stool was swiveled around, so there was nothing subtle about Legget's staring. Warren shifted his weight and looked down at his drink, rolling the glass between his palms. He stayed that way for what he felt was a minute, then glanced up. Legget was still staring.

What did he want? Warren wondered.

He tossed off his drink and savored the feeling the smooth liquor left in its wake as it made its way down to the empty pit of his stomach.

At last, Mara walked in. She was wearing a slight two-piece suit. The top acted as a lift for her full, bare breasts, outlining them in glowing material. The bottom glowed, too, like a beacon, directing Warren's eyes to the vee her long legs formed. She looked around slowly, as if studying every person in the room, then turned back to the doorway and nodded.

Freddie walked in.

He was wearing a pith helmet, khaki short-sleeve shirt and shorts, and high lace-up army boots. An imitation elephant gun was slung over his shoulder.

Freddie glanced around, smiling amiably, then spotted Warren. Warren had expected to see Freddie jump, act nervous, or react in some definite way once he'd been seen, but Freddie only smiled and strolled over to his table.

"Hey, Howie. How you doin'? You should've called and told me you were coming. I'd have been here sooner," Freddie said, sitting down across from him. "Been waiting long?" he asked, unslinging the toy gun and passing it to Mara.

Warren's left hand clamped tighter around the handle of the gun resting in his lap. He said nothing and glared at Freddie.

"Something wrong?"

"You know what's wrong." He lifted the gun and placed its butt firmly on the table, leveling the barrel squarely at Freddie's chest.

"Hey, take it easy. I *don't* know what's wrong. What's this all about?"

"You set it up. You got me fired."

Freddie's face was a mass of wrinkled confusion. "I *what?*"

"That big friend of yours in the Complex. Don't think I don't know all about it. Henri, right? Well, it worked. I've been fired and blackballed. I'll never get another job. I'll lose my crystal. My wife's never going to forgive me. And now it's your turn."

Freddie shook his head. "Now, wait a minute, Howie. I wouldn't do that to you. Something else is going on here."

Warren caught Mara's movement out of the corner of his eye, stiffened, prepared to fire at Freddie first, then anyone else who moved, but relaxed when he saw she was only moving out of his way.

"Come on, Howie. I want you to listen to me now. And I want you to listen very carefully," Freddie said. "I'm going to give you some money to hold you over for awhile."

The strain was too much for him. Warren was tired, feeling the effects of the alcohol. He moved to wipe his forehead without thinking, using his left hand, and felt a pin-prick—

Freddie stared at the needle that protruded from the side of Warren's neck. It had just appeared there in an instant. It was blue. Warren was dead even as his upper body fell forward and crashed down on the table top.

Freddie wheeled to his right and saw Legget standing by the bar, putting something into his pocket, trying hard to conceal a smug smile. He leapt to his feet and flung himself at the young man. He never landed a blow; three big men who had seen the entire situation unfold held him back before he could do any harm.

Legget looked like a frightened rabbit.

"What the hell did you do *that* for?" Freddie shouted.

"He was gonna *kill* you!" Legget whined.

"Him?! Are you crazy? *Him?*"

Legget bobbed his head. "He had a gun! You saw!"

"Yellow needles," Mara said. She stood beside Warren's still-warm body, holding his gun out in her palm.

Freddie glared at Legget. "Stupid! How could you be so fucking stupid! Have you got any idea what you just did?"

Legget's fear was mounting, his eyes darting, checking out the crowd, looking for an exit. "I . . . I. . . ."

Freddie shook his head. He felt like crying. Shit. He would have to feed Legget to the police. There was no sense in taking chances anymore. If Warren had told him the truth, then someone had set him up, gotten him fired, Freddie realized. He didn't want any of his affairs investigated. Especially by the police.

Only two people could have done this to Warren: Mara or Dennis. It was that simple. One or the other. Mara could have done it with one phone call to Henri, but Lange. . . .

"He's back," Mara whispered in his ear. "Lange is back."

"I know," Freddie said. "We ought to warn Johnson."

"If it's not already too late," she said.

"Call the police, and I'll try Johnson."

She nodded and walked away. Freddie watched her glide out of the lounge, her cat-like movements still graceful but no longer alluring—more threatening than anything else.

It could have been Lange, he thought. But it could have been Mara.

He despised Legget. He knew he couldn't do anything until he figured out which one it was—Mara or Dennis. And until he did, he'd have to walk carefully, with his eyes and ears wide open, attuned to the slightest clue or hint. It would be one or the other.

If only Legget had waited. The dolt—there'd been no need to kill Warren. He'd had information that could have helped.

He got up to try to get Johnson on the phone.

29

Dennis wasn't impatient. He had parked his car by the curb, two houses away from Oleo Johnson's house. It was getting late, and Dennis was getting hungry, but it was well worth waiting for. Johnson hadn't come home from work yet, even though the stock market had closed five hours ago. He had no idea as to where Johnson might be, nor did he care. Sooner or later Johnson would come home and, when he did, Dennis would be waiting. He had already done the hard part of putting his plan into motion; waiting was easy.

He took his eyes off the long, low, white house for enough time to reach in back to the table and locate a stimulant. He popped the small pill into his mouth and swallowed it dry, hoping it would take care of his hunger as well as his drowsiness, then turned back to his vigil.

Johnson might have been warned, but Dennis was willing to take that chance. There were only two people who knew he was back from Mexico City—Howard Warren, if he'd been able to figure it out, and Mary White.

Poor Mary, he thought. Johnson had gotten her, all right, in his inimitable fashion. Strapped her into a crystal-update chair, had her crystal being constantly updated while he slashed and cut her to shreds. When she woke up from the reconstruction, she carried the scars of the incident in her memory.

She had told him all about it when he'd called, right after he'd made the call to Howard Warren's superviser.

Warren had been fired—of that, Dennis was certain. He figured Warren had most probably gone home, then gone to Bentwell's or to Johnson's office. One or the other. It really made no difference. Dennis had set up Warren's being fired so that it would look like Freddie had engineered the whole thing. He hoped that was what Warren had assumed.

What he did from that point on made little difference to Dennis.

Dennis could kill him if and when he wanted to, pick his own time and place. The man's crystal had been repossessed, and that was all that mattered. If Warren were hit by a car, fell victim to a maniacal brawl in a bar, stepped in front of a police riot gun, or even died of natural causes, it still didn't matter. Dennis harbored no hatred for the man—just a refined feeling of revulsion. There was no need to kill him— nature or fate would do that. But it was reassuring to know that no matter how he died, Warren would never live again.

He felt he owed the man at least that much.

He was sure Freddie would have been alerted by Warren, either by an appearance for a confrontation, or by phone if he had seen that Dennis was behind his being fired. Dennis didn't care if Freddie knew or not, but it would be nice if he did. The time Dennis would take getting around to Freddie would give Freddie time to sweat. The longer Dennis took, the more Freddie would sweat.

But Johnson was altogether different. Different

steps had to be taken. From what he knew about Johnson, he had a pretty good idea as to how to take care of him.

Johnson was the kind of person who would never die unless he had to. Centuries ago, long before reconstruction was feasible, Johnson would have sought to live forever by becoming a legend. He would have probably been a murderer, Dennis thought, choosing his victims at random, killing them horribly, perhaps sexually assaulting them, then mutilating their bodies. There would have been no rhyme or reason to his selection of victims; there rarely was in the case of any psychopath. The police would have been powerless, unable to stop him, unable to find a pattern in the killings, knowing that the only way they would catch him would be by catching him in the act. He was the type that would have killed just for the blood lust and joy of killing.

And if there was one thing about him which Dennis was certain of, it was his reluctance to die. He had enough money for five crystals, five reconstructions, and still have plenty left over to indulge himself in his esoteric sexual tastes. He could afford to take his next life off, use it as a vacation, become one of the superslick, then use his following life to work and keep his credit level up.

Yes, Dennis thought, Johnson doesn't want to die.

And that made the particular method of dealing with his elimination very fitting. It had grown out of Dennis's long business relationship with him and his knowledge of the man.

There was a trick to it, though. Timing.

The stimulant was starting to take effect and Dennis was relieved. Breaking into the house hadn't been difficult, but it had been draining. His system had been keyed up, prepared to face Johnson if he'd arrived home early. He'd brought the right tools for the job and had altered the unit easily. It had taken a little longer than Dennis had liked, but it hadn't mattered since Johnson still wasn't home. If Johnson had walked in and surprised Dennis while he'd been working on the unit, Dennis had his gun right by his side, loaded with blue needles. He was glad for the extra surge of energy the pill was giving him.

The car. There it was. Dennis could see it in the console's rear monitor. Dennis started his car and pressed for manual control. The whole thing had to be timed just right.

Johnson's car was traveling slowly, going no more than forty kph. Dennis gripped the hand controls and readied himself. The stimulant helped increase his awareness and helped him see Johnson's car as if it were traveling at half its speed. He was ready.

Johnson's car passed Dennis.

Now! Dennis thought.

He swung out behind him and roared into the driveway right behind Johnson. He leapt out of the car and was by Johnson's door before the roof had slid half-way back, before Johnson knew what was happening.

Dennis smiled calmly, gun in hand, pointing through the glass window at Oleo's long, large, horsey head.

Oleo looked terrified at first, then slowly, a sheepish little-boy grin appeared on his face, as if Dennis had caught him with his hands in the cookie jar. He pressed the exit button and the doors slid upward and into the roof.

"Shoot," Oleo said.

"What's your rush?" Dennis asked. "You took your time with Mary. And with Kira. In fact, you never did it quickly."

Johnson's grin turned into a full smile. "Funny, Dennis. Cute."

"Yeah, cute."

"If you're not going to shoot me, then get out of my way. I'm tired and I've got a lot of things to do," Oleo said.

Anger whipped through Dennis like a hurricane, increased in force and intensity by the stimulant. His finger involuntarily tightened on the trigger but he managed to regain his composure in time to stop the action. He lashed out with his left hand, slapping Oleo's sunken cheek with the back of his hand. His hand stung.

"Show a little respect, Johnson. If not for me, then for this gun. Or I'll kill you."

"Well? What are you waiting for?"

Dennis thrust the gun forward so the barrel touched Oleo's nose. The pores on his face leaked sweat. "I don't like guns, Johnson, and I'm in no rush. You may be, but I'm not. You see, I'm saving you for last. I'm going to let you watch the others die, one by one, and let you try and figure out how to stop me. When I'm done with them, I'm coming after you. And it won't be clean and fast, like it would be with this," Dennis said, pressing the barrel harder against Oleo's nose.

Johnson's smile faded as he met Dennis's eyes. "Nice. But not nice at all. You made your point."

"Good."

Dennis kept the gun leveled at Johnson as he backed away and got into his car. The coordinates had already been entered into the automatic guidance system—all he had to do was close the car up and press for automatic control.

The car pulled out of the driveway and sped off down the road. Dennis immediately lunged for the box on the table, withdrew a tranquilizer, and washed it down with a long, deep swallow of mescanol.

He knew that by the time he got home Oleo Johnson would be dead. He gritted his teeth; the pill had not taken care of his hunger. He would go home, eat, then do some more research in the book.

Oleo sat in his car, shivering, teeth chattering, mind racing. Muscles in his arms twitched in time to some unconscious internal rhythm, jumping involuntarily, spasming their reaction to having been silenced by necessity. He absently rubbed his arm, as if the rubbing could smooth the muscles like rumpled sheets on a bed. His arm felt cold through his shirt.

He was queasy, and felt very let down. His body had screamed out its desire to move out of the way of Lange's gun, to slap it away with a hand, to hit him in the groin, to kick his head like a ball or a clump of blood-filled dirt. But his mind had shouted orders to his body to keep it from committing suicide. His muscles hadn't known that Lange could and would have pulled that trigger instantly, but his mind had. And now it was paying the price as his body went through the actions he had denied it earlier.

His mind replayed the confrontation over and over, trying to figure out why Dennis hadn't simply killed him while he had the chance. Lange's cool had run deep and led Oleo to believe that he could have meant what he said. Oleo would be the last to go.

He smiled, shook himself as a dog would, then swung out of the car seat easily. He was a little unsteady on his feet, but he felt better than he had sitting.

To hell with him, Oleo thought. Let him play his games. I'll be ready for him. Or whatever he's got planned. If and when he ever shows up again.

He walked to the front door and unlocked it. As the door clicked open, starting to slide on its tracks, he immediately realized his mistake and leapt to the side to avoid the shock wave and concussion from the bomb blast. Nothing happened externally; fiery adrenaline flowed internally. A chill ran down his back. He hadn't given any consideration to booby traps—his whole house could have been altered, or any unit inside it.

The whole house could be a death trap.

And then he remembered; Lange had pulled out behind him just a few houses away. And that meant that Lange could have been by, around, or inside the house all afternoon.

His phone was ringing.

Go inside and answer it? Not nice. Not nice at all.

Shit.

Whoever was calling would have to wait. He shook his head slowly, staring at the tiny colored pebbles that had been permanently frozen into position by the concrete of his front steps, trying to muster the courage to enter the house and get it over with. A car drove by, slowed opposite his driveway, then continued on down the street. It looked like Lange's car, but he couldn't be sure. Still, he realized he was no safer outside than inside.

The phone still rang.

Not nice at all, Oleo thought.

He would have to go inside and take his chances. Even if the house had been rigged and did manage to kill him, there was still his crystal. He would have his chance for revenge; he wouldn't actually die.

He swallowed with difficulty, squared his narrow shoulders, took a deep breath, and walked into the entrance foyer, expecting an immediate, painful death.

He opened his eyes.

Nothing had happened.

Maybe he was just jumpy. Yeah. Maybe Lange had been bluffing, trying to get him to lose control so he would have an excuse for pulling the trigger. And maybe not.

Check the crystal, he thought, then answer the blasted phone. If Lange destroyed it, then get out of the house, get to a Center, get the crystal replaced, update it, and keep it at the Center.

Yeah. The crystal first.

He walked into his bedroom, ignoring the invisible daggers, the nonexistent bombs, the heatless flames, and glanced at the crystal.

It hadn't been harmed. It sat there, sparkling like a deep, dark ruby, like crystalline blood. He sat down in its attached chair mechanism, swung the clear helmet down over the top of his head to update the crystal—just in case Lange did somehow get to him before he got another chance to update it.

He pressed the button.

The criss-crossing lasers sizzled through the top layer of hair, then flesh, then bone, then finally, brain tissue. The beams met at billions of intersections, mapping every newly-charred synapse, every newly-destroyed chemical interaction, burning their ways through Oleo's skull, cooking it from the inside and outside. The beams did the same thing to the crystal that they had done to the head that had once belonged to Albert "Oleo" Johnson.

30

Dennis opened the front door to his house, stepped inside, then froze. Something was wrong. He could sense it, like a dog who cocks his ear at some unheard sound. The door closed slowly behind him and he remained where he was, poised, coiled, ready to leap, to fall and roll to make himself a harder target. His eyes darted from side to side, taking in everything and nothing. There was someone else in the house. He was certain. He could feel the presence.

He eased the needle gun from his pocket and held it in a sweating hand. Who was it? Howard Warren? No; he realized Warren wouldn't try anything like this. That left Mara and Freddie. They were certainly more likely choices than Oleo Johnson. The late, great Oleo, Dennis thought.

He moved forward slowly, knees bent, head low, setting each foot down firmly, being sure of his balance before, during, and after each step. When he came to the opening in the right wall for the living room, he stopped, lay down flat, and cautiously peered around the corner and into the room. No one was there, but someone had fixed a drink and had left the bottle out.

Left the bottle out?

He heard noises coming from the kitchen.

Dennis stood, slipped the gun into his pocket, rubbed his face with his hands, then calmly walked into the kitchen. Kira was sitting in the breakfast nook, eating. She looked up at him as he crossed the room, then back to her food as he sat opposite her.

He'd figured it was her once he heard the noise and saw the bottle left out and uncorked. But what the hell was she doing here? She was supposed to be in Mexico City, in the hotel suite, waiting for his return. He realized then that she wasn't going to give him the eight days he had left of the ten, that she probably figured he didn't want to quit. She'd already given up on him.

He smiled awkwardly, unsure of what to say. He was still on edge; his nerves were still raw from the stimulant and the tranquilizer. The day's events were clear in his mind; each action and each motion taken was clearly imprinted on his memory. Somehow, Kira's presence jarred with the reality of what he had done.

"Hello," he said. The word sounded foolish, hung in the air between them, left a bad taste in his mouth.

She looked up at him as if just realizing he was there. "Hi."

"When did you get in?"

"A few hours ago."

A few hours ago? Why hadn't she called to tell him? He would have been at the airport to meet her; he could have driven her home. But why the hell did she have to come home now? Why couldn't she have waited a few more days? Given him a chance to deal with Freddie and Mara? He had more research to do in the book, and a lot of details needed to be worked out.

His hunger was bothering him. He shrugged, got

up, walked over to the terminal, and ordered a light supper. He would be able to think with some food in him.

"I thought we agreed that you would wait for me at the hotel," he said, leaning against the counter, arms tightly folded.

"I was, but it got old, fast," she said, not looking in his direction.

She wasn't telling him the truth. He could hear it in her voice, see it in the way she refused to look into his eyes while she spoke. Something was bothering her and she wanted to talk about it. It had to be important. Dennis could tell. It was over. He was in no rush to hear it, though. The words would cut him off from her and sever the relationship, chop him away from the one person who really meant something to him. Even these last few moments were precious. Until she actually told him, he could lie to himself with practiced ease, fool himself into believing that she still felt the same way he did. His hope was all he had left.

The food unit chimed softly and he bent over and reached to remove the plate. The roast beef was too well done, but it was hot, and he was too hungry to adjust the program and let it try again. He got a glass of fruit juice and carried it and the plate over to the nook.

Kira was done eating, and slowly sipped her drink.

Here it comes, he thought. He sat down opposite her.

"I can't stand it anymore," she said into her glass.

Dennis chewed the rubbery roast beef, resolved not to help or make it easy for her. She took another sip from her glass and set it down firmly, with finality. Maybe he should have told her why he had wanted to come back to the city. It might have made a difference; she might have understood more about him.

"We're like dinosaurs," she said to the table,

"hanging on long after our time. Most of our kind have been dead for longer than I can remember. We're anachronisms."

He swallowed and set down the fork. He picked up his glass and leaned back on the high-backed bench, his hunger engulfed by the large pit of emptiness he felt. "How long did it take you to figure that out?" he asked.

"What does *that* mean?" she asked, looking into his eyes for the first time.

"Nothing. Never mind. It's not important."

"If it wasn't important, then why did you say it?"

"Please, Kira, I don't want to fight now."

"You know, I thought I understood you, Dennis. I really did."

And this was how it was going to end. In a fight, a misunderstanding. Dennis took a sip from his glass. The juice was tart and he set it down beside his plate. He couldn't let it end like this, arguing over things that were trivial or that had nothing to do with him.

"Why did you come back now?" he asked.

"I was bored."

She was lying. He'd had enough of the meandering conversation. No more verbal sparring, no more talking around the point; it was far too late for that.

"You may have been bored, but that wasn't why you came back. You could have gone to your parents' place. You could have found someone in the hotel to keep you amused or occupied. You could have done ... something, anything at all, but you came here. And you came here for a reason. What is it?" he asked.

She said nothing.

"Why don't you tell me? It'll make it easier if you do. You owe me at least that much."

She looked confused. "Why do *you* think I came back?"

He sighed and rubbed his face, then placed his

elbows on the table and looked her straight in the eyes. "To tell me that it's over. That you don't want to give me the eight days."

She shook her head as though she was tired. "Dennis, your fucking insecurities are going to kill me. You haven't listened to one word I've said, have you?"

"Of course I listened."

"No, you didn't. Now *listen* to me. We live in a world that's changing—sometimes fast, sometimes slow. Marriage is treated like a fashion; I can understand a lot of your fears—people's attitudes toward marriage can change as quickly as hair styles or clothing. Very few people are what I consider really married—they have no intention to stay that way. When I called us dinosaurs, I meant what I said; this isn't a casual relationship for us. We didn't get married just so we could go through the excitement and bitterness of a divorce. We're not that kinky. We need each other. I'm not going to leave you. There's no reason why I should."

But there was, Dennis thought. If she knew why he'd insisted on leaving Mexico City to "straighten out" his affairs, she might feel differently. But she didn't know. Or did she? Maybe that was why she'd come home so soon, not waited for him as they'd planned. Or maybe, he hoped, she considered the eight day trial period over. Could she be that sure of her feelings? Could she be that sure what had happened in the small white room?

"I don't understand," Dennis said. "I'm glad you're home, but there's still something wrong—something you don't want to talk about. You're not telling me what it is. You could have waited. . . ."

"No, I couldn't have waited any longer." She sighed and moved her shoulders a few centimeters in a little shrug. "All right, there is something I wanted to know about, and I still do. After you left, all I could think about was what happened in the Center that night they . . . killed me."

"Oh."

"I want you to tell me what really happened. All of it. It's eating away at me. I couldn't sleep after you left. I have to know."

"That doctor of yours must have explained it to you."

"She did, but I want to hear it from you. I can't stand it anymore. She told me some of the physical things that were done to me, but I don't know what it was all about. Why did they do it, Dennis?"

He sighed and leaned back, afraid at first to recount what had happened. He didn't want to dig into those memories, face the part of himself that had died along with Kira, but he realized he would have to. He knew what it had been about, and she wanted to know.

He started slowly and told her about some of the people involved, the way Freddie had reacted when Dennis had refused his offers of partnership, the way Mara harassed him when he started talking to a potential angel, the way Freddie had reacted when Dennis had offered to cover for him with Bentwell.

He told her about Mary White, and how he'd wanted to set her up with Warren but had to settle for Johnson, and how Warren and Johnson had ended up working Kira over together. He figured that everyone involved must have sunk a lot of money into the setup, or that they had some help from someone pretty high up in the Complex.

He explained it to her the way he saw it—as an attempt to push him out of the business. He also pointed out that if they had only waited a few weeks, he would have probably quit the business on his own, without any outside interference.

"My God, Dennis. These people are animals!"

He shrugged. "Maybe."

"There's no doubt in my mind," she said, her face showing her inner upset and distress. "If they did that to us, then what are *you* doing here? You said you had to tie up some loose . . . oh, my God! Don't!"

"Don't what?"

"You're . . . you're going to kill them? You've come back to get them. There aren't any loose ends."

He looked away from her, knowing he was confirming her conclusion by saying nothing, yet unable to explain clearly why he had to do it. She hadn't known before, and if she had stayed in the hotel, then this confrontation might never have taken place.

"Do you want to make it worse? You'll be just as bad, just as sick as they are. If you go through with this you'll never be the same. You're not like that, Dennis."

He looked at her. "You're wrong. I am like that. And more. I'm already like them. It's too late—I can't stop now." He pushed his plate away. "Johnson's already dead. Warren's either dead, or as good as dead."

She blanched, the blood draining from her cheeks and lips; she looked deathly pale.

"It's too late, Kira. We can't ever go back to where we were. That part of our lives is over. It's as dead as you were when Johnson and Warren were finished with you. It'll never be the same.

"You're not the same person you were when we got married; time, disillusionment, money, and your reconstruction changed you. Our relationship can't go back to being what you want, to how you remember it. That part of our lives is over. Over and done with.

"Now is the time we've got to face who we are, what we mean to each other, where we've been, what's happened to us, where we're going. We're in a relationship, not a state of stability," he said.

She said nothing.

"We've got to grow, Kira. Grow and learn to live with each other as we are, not as we were."

She looked at him accusingly, head lowered, eyes fixed steadily on his. "You've made your point. Are you going to go through with this?"

"I don't see where I have a choice at this point. I couldn't stop now even if I wanted to," he said, hoping she wouldn't press it further.

She shook her head, then got up from the nook. She took her plate and glass to the cleaner and placed them inside. Dennis watched her move, afraid that with each step she took she got further and further away from him and the reality of their relationship.

"Face it, Kira. Face the truth. Look at what our marriage has become. If you don't, you'll spend the rest of your life lying to yourself, fantasizing about our being together, about what might have happened. Look at me. Look!"

She turned and looked. She was biting her lower lip; silent tears ran down her cheeks. He got up from the nook and crossed the room to her side, standing there, trying to find more words that could help her accept what had happend and what they were.

"I don't like what I've become any more than you do. I can't fight it, and I refuse to run away from it. I'll deal with it, the same way I'm dealing with the fact that you're reconstructed, and the fact that I had a breakdown. I don't like it, and I wish it never happened, but it did. And if we're going to stay together, we're both going to have to fight these things and not let them get in the way."

She started sobbing, then, and threw her arms around him. "Dennis," she said through racking sobbing breaths.

"We're going to make it," he said, as much for himself as for her.

He just wished she'd stayed in Mexico City for a

few more days, far away from the things he had to do. He would have to learn how to put her out of his mind until it was over. Lying to her would have been so much easier if he didn't love her.

31

Dennis woke up and eased out of bed slowly, careful not to wake Kira. It was mid-morning and he was tired, but there was work to do—work he didn't want Kira to see. He grabbed his clothes and headed for the bathroom. After washing up, he dressed, then went down the hall to his den. He pulled the old, leather-bound book out from the shelf and set it down on his desk. He sat down and turned to the index and found the page number for atropine.

Atropine is normally extracted from the nightshade plant, *Atropa Belladonna*. Belladonna is an important name to keep in mind, since tincture and extract of belladonna are still in use. Getting atrophine directly from the plant is the most desirable method since this leaves no trace of where and how the user has obtained the chemical. (For extracting techniques, see p. 190). Some pharmaceutical preparations use belladonna, but the quantity and purity is usually far too small to be of use. Other chemicals may be substituted within the atropine family, but none are as easy to find.

Normal hallucinogens which do not block the function of acetycholine can be used, but of course the results will be different: the victim's central nervous system, CNS, will not be impaired as it is with the parasympatholytic atropine group. . . .

He closed the book and leaned back in his chair. Atropine would have been just the thing he needed. Dennis knew that his whole plan of dealing with them rested on getting his hands on the drug. But if getting it meant risking everything, he would find a suitable replacement for atropine. He wasn't about to break into the pharmacy in the Center just to get the drug —not when there was so much at stake.

Perhaps he would have to revise his plan. It was complicated and very fitting, but it did rest on too many small details. The plan was too fragile—it no longer seemed workable. Getting them to take the drug, putting them in a swimming pool, then tossing in huge amounts of sulfuric acid seemed like a nice way for them to go but more and more infeasible.

Maybe mescanol would be enough. Of course, both Freddie and Mara would know they were taking it—they would recognize its effects immediately and know how to deal with it. But that wouldn't be that bad, either. He didn't want the drug to do the damage—he wanted to save that action for the tremendous reaction that would occur when he tossed in the sulfuric acid. All the drug was supposed to do was disorient them and make them receptive. Perhaps a mild hypnotic would do.

He decided to check the drugs he had available to him in the house, find out what effects different dosages would have. Maybe he could find something that would work just as well.

He found what he wanted in the drug dispenser in the main bathroom. Common chloral hydrate. He'd looked it up in the book and found that the hypnotic dose was one gram. The capsules were 0.5 grams each, so he put four of them in his pocket. He could get Freddie and Mara to swallow them without too much problem—he couldn't foresee them refusing if he pointed a gun to their heads.

The only problem now, though, was getting the acid, finding the swimming pool where no one else would be hurt, and getting close enough to them so he could point the gun.

Dennis drove down the street slowly, using his car's manual controls. He stopped half a block from the Franks' small house and walked the rest of the distance. The sun was setting behind the row of houses, casting long shadows across the sidewalk and the street. The front of the house was landscaped like a lush tropical garden. Dennis had no trouble finding a clump of trees on the front lawn that would give him good cover. He walked over the grass, hiding behind small bushes and trees. He figured he wouldn't have to wait more than two hours. Two hours. It was worth it.

The sun had set and stars lit the sky by the time the front door cracked open. Dennis eased the gun out of his pocket and sighted down its barrel to the door. It opened a little more and Freddie appeared, head only, held at an angle, glancing around the doorframe, trying to spot anyone who might be waiting.

Dennis was glad. Freddie was sweating it out just as Dennis had hoped he would, worrying about where and when Dennis would make his move, knowing full well what was going on, being as cautious as his limited frontal lobes would allow. Dennis kept the gun centered on his head, on his pure and innocent baby face.

He came out onto the porch alone, walked down the winding steps to the garage, then pressed the button on the wall. The garage door opened and Dennis heard the whine of the car's electric motor coming up to speed. He continued to sight down the barrel to the small of Freddie's back.

He hadn't managed to get the acid—the whole idea was out of the question, now. Kira would be troubled, anxious, nervous, edgy, waiting for it to be over. He'd decided to eliminate the full-blown plan he'd thought up and concentrate on getting Freddie and Mara some other way.

Freddie went back up the steps, glancing around furtively. He stopped at the front door and called inside to Mara. She appeared behind him and they closed up the house.

Dennis dropped them both in their tracks as they walked down the steps. It had gone smoothly—as smooth as Freddie's makeup, as flawless as Mara's reconstructed body. He smiled at the two yellow needles sticking into their unconscious forms.

He left them lying on the steps while he retrieved his car. He walked slowly, calmly, as if taking a stroll on a balmy evening. He drove his car into their driveway, then loaded them into the back. He pressed their car's park button and it returned to the garage, shut itself off, and closed the garage door.

That was it. They were *his* now.

Dennis let the car get sixty kilometers outside the city before taking over manual control. He pulled off the main road and found a dirt road. He followed this for several kilometers, then pulled off on a grassy shoulder. The moon had risen and bathed the wooded area in an eerie light. He opened the doors and sat there, calmly waiting for the stun needles to wear off. They would come around soon enough, and he was in no rush. He tried not to think of Kira, about her waiting at home, and turned his mind to working out the details of what had to be done.

It was a good, solid alternate plan, though less dynamic than the sulfuric acid one.

Mara stirred, then opened her eyes. She saw Dennis and tried to smile, but her nervousness and fear betrayed her. "What next?" she asked.

"You'll see soon enough. Be patient."

"I'm sure."

Dennis eased back in his seat and waved the gun around. "Seen Howard Warren lately?"

"He's dead. Some schmuck *he* hired shot him," she said, shrugging at Freddie's insensate form.

Dennis smiled. Then all that was left was the Franks. What was taking Freddie so long to come out of the stun needle's effect? "Shake him a little. Wake him up."

She shook her head. "Not yet. I want to talk to you."

"Oh?"

She nodded. "Without him hearing."

"Go ahead. Talk."

"How's Kira?"

Dennis was getting angry. For the first time since he'd started taking care of them all, he felt a deep, volatile anger. The muted sense of accomplishment and satisfaction that everything was going well had been just that—and nothing more. It had been a job, a responsibility; killing Johnson hadn't been involving. He hadn't even been there for his death. It had just been getting rid of an annoying person who had gotten in the way.

"She's fine."

"Not many relationships can survive when a person's been reconstructed, you know, never mind what you two went through."

"What's the point, Mara?" Dennis asked, his patience wearing thin.

She shrugged and her breasts moved in the moonlight. "Sex, Dennis. How's your sex life? I mean, Freddie over here—he's certainly no tiger, you know? If it wasn't for the people at Bentwell's—I mean, God! But there's no reason for you to suffer with Kira while she gets adjusted and learns how to trust you all over again. How's she feel about the business you're in?"

"I'm not a procurer anymore," he said angrily.

"Oh, you're not? What's this revenge trip all about then, huh? You probably told her you were quitting and she believes you and everything's fine and you figure you'll start getting laid again, right? She doesn't believe you, though. She'll never believe you didn't have something to do with the setup."

"Shut up."

"No matter what she says, she'll never believe you. Never."

"I said, shut up!"

She shook her head. "Don't be stupid, Dennis. We're both good-looking people. Let's dump this—this blob and start out together. You and me."

"Shut *up!*"

"Don't you need someone who respects you, who can relate to your work, who would—"

He leapt to his feet, a deep low growl starting from deep within his throat. He had dropped the gun. He was at Mara's side before she'd had a chance to move, to realize what was happening. He picked her up with one hand, a hand clamped around her throat, and flung her from the car like a rag doll.

She landed with a dull thud, and bounced once. She groaned and rolled onto her side, trying to get to her feet. She never made it.

Dennis grabbed her by the ankles and leaned back, dragging her a short distance. Then, still dragging her, he put more power into pulling and started moving in a circle. Mara's body lifted from the ground as he made the circle tighter and tighter and increased his speed, acting as a pivot, leaning far back to keep his footing and balance. He ignored her screams, her pleading, her whining and begging to be put down.

Still holding her by the ankles, her head rushing less than half a meter above the ground, he smashed her into a nearby tree. Immediately, blood splattered his clothes, his face, his hands, the tree trunk, and the ground beneath her body.

So much for the plan, for the atropine, for the hypnotic.

He went back to the car and up its ramp to stare at Freddie Frank. Areas of Dennis's skin were wet beneath his clothing—wet with Mara's blood. There was no time left for fun and games, for cat and mouse, for retribution; even by the loose laws which governed Dennis's actions, he knew he had just murdered. If Mara's body were found, it wouldn't be even close to an accidental death, as he knew Johnson's had been.

He shook Freddie to rouse him from the effects of the needle. Freddie stirred, rubbed his eyes with balled fists, then opened them. When he did, he wished he'd kept them shut. Even in the dim, silvery moonlight, Dennis could see the blood pounding and jumping in the veins in Freddie's neck, the sweat beading over his upper lip.

"Then it *was* you," Freddie said. "It was you all along."

Dennis's forehead furrowed and he shook his head. "What are you talking about?"

"Where's Mara?"

"Over there," Dennis said, jerking his head in her general direction.

"Is she. . . ."

"Dead? Yes, she's dead."

"Oh." Something happened to Freddie as he sat there. Confidence and self-composure leaked out of him like a balloon slowly leaking air. Dennis thought he looked pitiful, ridiculous in those jodhpurs, riding boots and polo shirt.

"It's all over, Freddie. I knew it wasn't your idea to do that to Kira—it couldn't have been. You don't have the imagination; you never did. You and I've been through a lot together, coming up the hard way, fighting for everything we got, having to struggle. I knew it was Mara behind it all."

Freddie nodded absently, eyes clouded over, unfocused, liquid in the moonlight. "Yeah, you're right. It was her. It was all her. But I guess I did go along with her."

Dennis moved closer and squatted down to be on Freddie's eye level. "Hey, don't blame yourself. If she'd approached me a long time ago instead of you, I would've taken her up in a minute." He rested a hand on Freddie's shoulder. "Don't worry about it. I understand what happened. I just had to stop her before she killed me, too."

"And she tried to get me, too, Dennis!" Freddie said. "There was a point when I wasn't sure if it was you or her. Howard Warren showed up at Bentwell's and he pulled a gun on me. She'd set me up—got him fired so he'd think I did it to him."

"Hey, come on. Take it easy. Don't let her get to you anymore. It's better this way; you're free from her now."

Freddie looked deep into Dennis's eyes, confused. "I don't understand."

"It's all over, Freddie. We don't have to hate each other anymore. Mara's not coming back; Oleo's not coming back; Warren's not coming back. It's just me and you, just like the old days," Dennis said, a soft, tender smile on his face.

Freddie swallowed once, then took a little breath of air, as if afraid it might be his last if Dennis saw him breathing. "Let's get it over with."

"Get what over with?" Dennis asked.

"I'm the only one left. Do it. Just do it quick."

"I already told you: It's over. I'm not going to kill you. If I wanted you dead, you'd have been dead a long time ago."

Freddie shook his head. "I don't get it. If you're not going to kill me, then what's this all about?"

Dennis calmly picked up the needle gun he'd dropped when dealing with Mara, stood, then slipped it into his pocket. "I didn't want you, Freddie. But I had to take both of you at the same time. If I hadn't, you'd think I was still out to kill you. All I wanted was her. I meant what I said when I told you it was over."

Freddie shook his head slowly.

"Come on," Dennis said. "We've got some hard and dirty work ahead of us. And it's going to take most of the night."

Freddie stood, the confusion he felt making creases and lines in his face the makeup couldn't cover. "What are you talking about?"

"There are two shovels in the trunk. Let's get to work." Dennis walked down the ramp and around to the trunk. "Aren't you going to help?"

Freddie started as if someone had pricked him with a needle. "Help?"

"Yes, help. Mara's got to be buried. We can't just leave her body on the ground, can we? She made enough trouble for us both while she was alive—let's not give her the chance while she's dead. We've got to make sure no one finds her body for a long, long time. Without the genetic pattern from her body, her crystal's worthless. She's not coming back, Freddie. Let's keep it that way."

Freddie walked down the ramp and toward Dennis as if he were dreaming. Dennis handed him a folding shovel and kept the one he'd intended for Mara. They walked into the woods for several meters;

Dennis led the way and stopped at a small clearing beneath a tall old elm.

"This looks like a nice soft spot, partner," Dennis said. He jammed the blade of the shovel into the earth. "Save all the grass. When we're done we can cover the dirt with it and in a few months there'll be no trace of our . . . handiwork."

Freddie stood motionless, staring in disbelief. Dennis carefully divided chunks of sod and moved them to one side. The black soil beneath smelled rich and humid, full of decay and life. He stopped after the fourth piece, knifed the shovel blade into the dirt, and leaned on its handle.

He looked at Freddie's round face, pale in the moonlight. "What's wrong?" he asked.

"Wrong?"

"Yeah, wrong. Why aren't you helping? Don't you like the idea?"

"What idea?" Freddie asked.

"Being partners. Fifty-fifty. With Mara out of the way, I thought. . . ." He motioned with his palm up.

"Are you serious?"

"Yes, I am." Dennis smiled. "What's to stop us?"

Freddie took a few moments to think it over, to try to get used to the idea. Going from sure death to instant partnership was a big conceptual leap for his expectations, and it took a few seconds for him to absorb and accept it. "Are you serious? Partners?"

Dennis nodded. "Yeah. Weren't you listening? I told you that I knew it was Mara. You and I don't have to hate each other anymore. You know that if I really wanted you dead, you'd be cold by now. What more do I have to do to convince you?"

A smile lit Freddie's face; only on him, it didn't quite look like a smile. "Nothing, partner. You just did."

He rammed the shovel into the ground and started clearing away the top layer of sod. Dennis worked alongside.

By the time the grave was dug deep enough to protect it from casual discovery and roving animals, they had worked out the fine points of their arrangement. As the evening passed, Freddie had loosened up and talked to Dennis, confiding the fears, the insecurities, the paranoia that living with Mara had created. He made it sound like a bad dream, something surreal, far removed from his own dreams of success.

"Let's get her," Dennis said, walking back toward the car.

Freddie followed.

Dennis was tired and dirty, but the stimulants he had taken were keeping him going. His hands were raw. When they reached Mara's body, he felt a little queasy; insects had discovered and claimed the remains. Dennis bent over and grabbed her hands.

"Take her feet," he said.

Freddie stood there, sickness overcoming him in a wave, rushing up from his stomach. He turned his head and vomited. Dennis waited until Freddie had stopped heaving, then asked him to help again. Freddie was weak, but he helped carry her to her grave in the woods.

Dennis dropped her into the deep hole unceremoniously, as if the body was no more than a sack of potatoes. Freddie lurched and almost fell in, too, as she was ripped from his grasp. Her body rested on the bottom in a way only the dead can achieve, arms and legs at impossible angles.

Dennis stood there looking down at her for a long, silent moment, then picked up his shovel. Freddie did the same.

Freddie bent over to take his first shovelful of earth, to start covering his horrible past, his naked fears. Dennis held his shovel at the very end of the handle and swung the blade's edge at Freddie's knees with all his might. The kneecaps snapped, cracked in the still night.

Freddie howled, collapsed to the ground, his broken knees no longer able to support his weight. He rolled, screaming in fear and pain. Dennis approached him and rolled him to the edge of the pit with his foot.

"It's the least I could do," Dennis said, drowned out by Freddie's agonized wails.

He kicked him into the grave.

Freddie's fall was cushioned by Mara's body, and his shrieks doubled in intensity and horror; he whined and howled, jabbering insanely, madly, clawing at the walls of dirt, pleading for pity, for mercy, trying to scramble up and out of the grave without the use of his broken legs. He couldn't reach the top without standing. And he could no longer stand.

Dennis bent over and took one last look, then picked up his shovel and starting throwing dirt in to fill the hole.

"No!" Freddie screeched.

Dennis smiled, said his silent yes, and continued his labor of love.

32

"Mescanol?" Kira asked from the bar.

"Sure." Dennis was lying on the suspensor couch, hands entwined behind his head, feet up on the coffee table, looking through the porch's glass doors at Mexico City's night lights. He felt at peace with himself; his mind no longer raced, planned, schemed. There were two days left to the trial period and he'd wanted to spend them with Kira, isolated and secure, cut off from everything their life had been.

She walked across the room, glasses in her hands, smiling. "I want you to try to relax. You've got to unwind."

He laughed softly. "Unwind? What's that?" he asked, sitting up to take the glass from her.

She'd poured him five fingers. He downed it in two swallows.

"Have you decided what you're going to tell Bentwell?" she asked, sitting beside him.

"No, not yet. There's still plenty of time." He rubbed his face then shook his head. "We should talk about it before I say anything more to him. It won't be procuring, but I will have to deal with the same group of people. And I will be making my living off procurers."

She sipped her drink. "Let's not talk about it now. If there's plenty of time, let's wait, enjoy what time together we've got."

He nodded. "Partnerships aren't something you can just jump into."

She leaned over and kissed his cheek. "Try to relax, will you? Let me get you another drink."

"No, I'm fine. You sit for awhile."

"Don't you worry about me. I'll get you another, but you've got to promise to take it a little slower, okay? It's mescanol—not water."

He nodded, starting to feel the first effects of the drink. "Okay."

He watched her slide glide across the floor, the liquid sparkling tiles, through the apparitions, the mist, the colored walls of air, to the bar. She squeezed a drink from the bottle and started back toward him. The flames, the heat, the stench of burning flesh followed. He looked away quickly, past the terrace, to the hot night outside the glass doors. She sizzled as she approached.

He heard the glasses being set down on the table before him and felt her settle in his lap. He looked up at her; the fire, like a corona, surrounded her head. She leaned over to kiss him. He managed not to cringe.

ABOUT THE AUTHOR

MICHAEL BERLYN was born in Brookline, Massachusetts and received a degree in Humanities and Science from Florida Atlantic University. He began writing at the age of fifteen and started concentrating on science fiction in his early twenties. Mr. Berlyn has held a variety of jobs, including pinball-arcade money changer, sales manager for a multi-million dollar corporation and electric violin player in a professional rock and roll band. For relaxation, Mr. Berlyn enjoys painting watercolors and listening to his vast music collection. His pleasure reading ranges from science texts, to mainstream literature to science fiction. He is currently living in West Palm Beach, Florida with his wife, the author M. M. McClung.

FANTASY AND SCIENCE FICTION FAVORITES

Bantam brings you the recognized classics as well as the current favorites in fantasy and science fiction. Here you will find the beloved Conan books along with recent titles by the most respected authors in the genre.